Kisses fr

and other stories

C.G. Harris

PublishNation
www.publishnation.co.uk

For Amaan, Eshaan and Aria-Rose

CONTENTS

Foreword

FOREWORD

I finished writing this collection of stories in a much different country to that in which I began; indeed, in many ways a different world. The Covid 19 pandemic has caused hardship and suffering throughout, even if one did not have the virus itself. As I write, we are all just easing our way back to normality or, at least, a new form of normality.

However, we have all been fortified by the efforts of those who put themselves at the forefront of the fight against the disease, for which we are grateful.

Throughout the lock-down I feel sure that reading will have been one of the pleasures that those in isolation have continued with, or taken up anew - along with a newfound enthusiasm for exercise! This being the case, I hope that readers of all persuasions will take great pleasure from this collection of 18 very different stories, which offer entertainment and escapism when required, even as we get back to the other things that we once took for granted.

C.G. Harris
June 2020

KISSES FROM THE SUN

Juan Luis Garcia Hernandez woke with murder on his mind. How do I know this? I answer simply: this morning, concerned, he told me so. Yet, even if he had not, there was a heat in his eyes and upon his brow that informed me of a troubled mind.

Now, let me say that although I but work as his foreman I have been his friend for some years and I cannot argue that such a frame of mind is a healthy one. I am sure that he himself was as much disturbed as I; it is not a thought that a respectable Spanish landowner such as himself would normally entertain. But he has a very young and lovely wife, and jealousy is an emotion not easily controlled.

We had breakfasted early together, as was our custom, whilst the sun rose up from the sea across the bay. I will say that our positioning for repasts is perfect, for the garden of Juan Luis is set amongst orange and olive trees and nestles on the cliff heights where one can look down upon the small town of Canos de Belleza. Indeed, this day, once we had eaten a simple breakfast of *tostada* with olive oil and drunk our coffee, served by the beautiful, slim, dark haired wife of which I speak, he took me by the arm, this tall, narrow man with the saddest of moustaches, and, placing his ivory Panama upright upon his head, walked me through a tiny grove to a stall whereupon we could sit and view the small town in its bleached and modest glory. Some distance below, the waves marched back and forth in their forlorn, unhurried way and we sat for some time unspeaking; eventually I saw that the rhythm of the seas dispelled something of his mood.

"Maria is a beautiful woman, is she not?"

This was undoubtedly the case and I replied without hesitation that indeed she was.

"And she is young, is she not? By this I mean, my friend, that she is considerably younger than I…"

This, too, was a fact I could not dispute and so I coughed and said:

1

"Yes, Juan Luis, she is beautiful and she is young – but you are rich," we laughed before I continued, "besides which, she loves you, I believe."

He did not look at me but nodded and replied: "She has some affection for me, I think it is so – I cannot say whether it is love."

"Love can take a man or a woman in many ways, and at different times and at any age; who is to say why one loves another?" I responded.

I watched as he held out his hands and turned them, first palm up, then down, and studied them closely. The wind moved but softly through the olive trees, yet when it did the branches shook; from between them the light from the morning sun, now bright and yellow, reached down and caressed my face.

At last, Juan Luis said, "I am not so young, my health is not good, my hair has gone and my ability to please a woman with it. I envy you, Ricardo, you retain your vigour; you are like a handsome bull, although one with sensibility, it is true."

"Why do you talk this way, Juan Luis?" I said.

"There are those who would love to please Maria in a way that I cannot." His eyes had regained that glowing heat and he stood and walked to the cliff edge; he motioned for me to join him. "See," he pointed to the far side of the bay, "there is a fine house."

It *was* a fine house. Large and whitewashed, it shone like a pearl set upon green velvet; the grounds led down to the azure sea; white to green, to blue.

"I know the house, Juan Luis, and so do you – it is that of Emiliano Ortega – not as rich as yourself perhaps," I shrugged, "but wealthy, it must be said."

"Yes, Ricardo; he too is a handsome man, with one eye on his wealth and the other, I fear, upon Maria. I watched closely those eyes as we sat at dinner together in *Casa de Comida Hermosa*, Maria and I. He was across the way and lounging at his ease alongside the bar – oh, you know how he has this arrogant way about him, he and his laughing *companeros* – and he raised his glass, one of many he had drunk, I am sure, in our direction. It was politely done, I grant you, but I did not disregard the fact that his face was flushed when he looked at Maria; it was not with the wine, Ricardo, it was..." Juan Luis lowered his voice, "It was with desire, Ricardo." He spat out the offending word.

I could not help but burst into laughter and Juan Luis' own face flushed, but with annoyance.

"Why do you laugh?!"

"Come, my friend, you cannot get angry at every man who looks at your wife!" I protested.

"There is more, Ricardo." His voice remained low.

"Yes?"

"Maria has been lying to me..." Juan Luis shook his head; it seemed to me to express not only sadness but a quiet disbelief that she should do so. I recalled how he had taken her from the *taberna* where she worked for money that kept the wolf from the door but little else, married her and gave her an enviable lifestyle; yet for some I knew that luxury could not assuage a certain restlessness of spirit – it is often the way, and of course she was young, with all the physical needs that youth requires.

I remained silent and waited for him to continue; for a woman to lie to her husband was not unheard of but in all cases for the husband it is a matter of respect and pride; in Juan Luis' case I could see that it was still more: there was a passion that surprised me in one of his advancing years.

"There was the time she was due at the house of her mother...she did not arrive. And then her sister was surprised when I asked how Maria's visit to *her* went; it did not occur. And have you noticed, my friend, there is a certain *alegria de la vida* about her person...a joy of life of which I am not the source, I fear. The eyes, they sparkle; the lips, they taunt me with secretive smiles; she hums the songs of love and desists when I am near."

I shook my head and did my best to reassure him that these were but the figments of an imagination fevered with love but he continued with some bitterness.

"There are rumours, Ricardo. The villagers, they avert their gaze as I pass, and they laugh at me, of that I am sure; and they are right to do so, for there is no such fool as an old fool who has more money than sense. But I will tell you this, my friend," he shook me from my complacency when he whispered: "I will kill the man that touches Maria."

3

Such vehemence startled me, it must be said, but he continued: "I must know, Ricardo. I *will* know."

I found myself leaning forward with all earnestness to ask: "And so, Juan Luis? What does this mean?"

In return, he stood and informed me that he had invited Emiliano to dinner that very evening.

*

La Cena is not the main meal of the day, this instead being the midday repast in our hot clime, so I was surprised when Juan Luis, having insisted I also attend, stated that the evening meal would be hosted earlier than is usual, around 6:00 pm. This he laughingly assured me would be a meal somewhat larger than customary to satisfy my appetite and with plenty of wine to loosen the tongue and any inhibitions; I assumed this to mean Emiliano's, not my own. I fear that my friend had but simple cunning; he would watch – as sharply as the eagle – for a sign, the slightest one, that Emiliano and Maria were more than mildly acquainted.

I pondered upon this as I sat on the veranda of my own modest villa during the heat of the day and looked out upon the old fishing town with its rough beauty; it was so very nearly quiet and lay like a sleeping, panting dog. The sun threw down its hazy heat and when I closed my eyes and raised them towards it the rays warmed my face. I found myself turning towards the crags and the villa above them in which Juan Luis, Emiliano, Maria and I would gather that evening.

Let me speak of Maria.

Of the dozen or so establishments where one could eat and drink the most popular was *La Taberna de los Sinvergüenzas*. This was indeed where the few scoundrels of the small town would gather for *tapas* hour and long after; the food was plentiful and inexpensive, the wine even more so, and it boasted the prettiest waitresses in Canos de Belleza – of these, Maria had been the most exquisite without a doubt. She bore attention with all good humour; her flashing, dark eyes could attract those young men she took a liking to, or repel those she did not. When Juan Luis and I, no scoundrels ourselves but attracted by laughter as we passed by – laughter that falsely insinuated itself within

4

Juan Luis that he was young again – entered the *taberna* Maria's teeth flashed in our direction. They were as white as her virgin blouse, which was nipped in at her waist, and her skirts flowed in colourful abandon as she whirled between the tables. I recall she was like a wild untamed bird, her raven hair flowing and her delicate hands swift and sure as she served; is there any wonder that Juan Luis would wish to capture and tame that bird, albeit with kindness? Myself, I felt then that no man could do so – better to appreciate her vigour, her magnificence, as one appreciates the plumage of such a bird before it vanishes among the trees.

One never truly knows another being, however; Maria was poor, and of a more practical turn of mind than I assumed. Juan Luis, through the force of personality that has made him a rich man, and, by the by, being the bearer of many gifts, took her for his wife; it has to be said that it was a willing arrangement with a coming to terms over many weeks. Juan Luis was besotted but happy and it is not for me to say that he should not be so.

Emiliano and I arrived together that evening at the gates of Casa Hernandez. By this, I mean that we stepped from our cars just as six chimes rose from the *iglesia* of the Virgen Del Carmen far below; when these sounds had ceased to hang in the air, which returned to a heavy stillness, we stepped forward and shook hands. I could not help but notice that Emiliano smiled at the sight of my vehicle, a small but perfectly formed Seat 600 which had seen better days, it has to be said, but which negotiates the steep and winding roads from the town with assuredness; I do not think I would place the same trust in the weighty, ostentatious Mercedes in which Emiliano arrived, which was vivid red in colour and comfortable but unwieldy.

I cannot say that I disliked Emiliano. In fact, I might say that we could have been friends. There was a mischievous swagger about him that I admired and which made me smile. He was younger than I by some five years or so, being in his thirties if my eyes did not deceive me, and although we were of the same frame, tall and heavy – substantial, one might call us – he was inclined to portliness whereas I, no doubt because of my work on the land, had no such fat upon me. Regardless, he was a handsome man with his long, dark, swept back hair and those dancing eyes.

I do not know under what pretext Juan Luis had requested the company of Emiliano – I suspect where business and money were concerned their interests converged, and of course for Emiliano the company of a voluptuous hostess is always worth cultivating. In addition, the generous hospitality of Juan Luis is well renowned; Emiliano, by all appearances, was not one to refuse such generosity.

The tall gates, which were metal-wrought, red and golden in the lowering sun, stood open and when we walked through them together Juan Luis was waiting to greet us. Maria stood by him and the light lustred her hair, making it fairer than I had ever seen it. She was tiny and elegant in a cool, white blouse and red cotton skirt; I noticed that Emiliano smoothed back his hair at this vision, then stepped forward and, after greeting Juan Luis warmly, rather quaintly bowed and took Maria's delicate hand, kissing the back of it lightly. He did not linger but I saw that Juan Luis watched closely; Maria herself was effervescent and sparkled as she always did when the centre of attention.

What can I say about that meal? It was both gay and fraught at once as we ate and conversed – and watched each other – and the shadows of the olive trees slowly lengthened, darkening the table at which we sat. Maria served us herself, Juan Luis dismissing the old *cocinera* for the evening once she had prepared the meal – for which I must give praise as there was an array of temptatious fish and fowl and abundant colourful vegetables which sat upon pristine white cloth; the wine flowed and it did not matter whether it was white or red, for there was a kind of abandon that seeped its way amongst us as we ate.

I found myself taking to Emiliano, with his charm and roguish wit, something which I had not expected, and I must admit that Juan Luis looked slow and aged beside this ebullience; yet I knew that Juan was a clever man – one did not become as rich as he without a certain sharpness and even ruthlessness when the need arose. He laughed when he felt he should, though smiled a little distantly when he did not approve of a joke, and all the while I could see that his eyes were on Maria. I had never seen her so enchanting and to me she appeared to sway and whirl with

6

gaiety as she refilled our glasses as soon as they emptied; she did this with the efficiency of the waitress she had once been and the assurance of the hostess she now was. The meal would have proceeded in this fashion with no ill effects apart from bloated stomachs and aching heads in the morning...but Maria let her hand rest lightly upon Emiliano's shoulder as she poured his wine; and his face glowed while she looked down and smiled upon him.

When I glanced at Juan Luis, I discerned no visible change. There was no frown, no pursed lip; his hand was steady as he raised his glass and he laughed at the next humorous sally of Emiliano's. Yet, knowing him as I do, I could sense a tautness about the line of his body; and his chin, of the weak kind that often belies a firmness of nature, for once had a jutting quality about it. He drank his glass to the full before he rose, and, inviting Emiliano to join him in discussing some business matters that he might find of interest, he suggested that they take their cigars and a bottle of his best *Mencia* to the seat overlooking the sea where they might talk peaceably. When I rose, Juan Luis placed his hand upon my arm and said in a carefree manner that I would only be bored at such talk. Uncorking the *Mencia,* he filled my own glass with the deep, red wine; it was peppery on the palate and, delighting in the aroma of sour cherry and pomegranate, I sat down again.

"Enjoy, my friend," he said. I watched as the pair strolled toward the olive grove, Emiliano the slightest bit unsteady on his feet.

When they had disappeared from view, Maria sat opposite me and for long moments we – she with her black eyes set upon my face, which must have reflected my troubled thoughts – sat in silence. In such quietude I imagined a scene, such a scene, whereby Juan Luis, satisfied that Emiliano was not only full of desire but had acted upon it, would, in slow, silent anger, inflamed within himself yet as placid without as a dove, stand beside Emiliano on that cliff edge. He would point out that white villa, in its pristine, pretty splendour, and Emiliano, intoxicated and delighted, and in his pride, would move forward to see it the better. He would be heedless of the rocks below upon which the waves, no longer languid, beat a rhythm more suited to jealousy

7

and death. And Juan Luis would step back behind Emiliano and push out his arm …

I, Ricardo, the handsome bull, began to shake and Maria reached out her hands and placed them over mine. I felt the coolness of them; my own were as heated as my doubting thoughts which, knowing me but recently and yet so very intimately now, she read and sought to dispel with her touch.

I thought of the death of one man who I did not really know, but also the long imprisonment which would follow of one who regarded me as his friend; I shook because these thoughts did not come naturally to me and I hated myself for them. Then I considered the fact that Maria and I would be together and, even more, with all the accompaniments of Juan Luis's wealth. Yes…yes, if we remain here quietly, with the wine and the wind and the kisses from the dying sun, it could be so. It was true after all, as I had told Juan Luis – was it but this morning? – that love may take a man at any age and at any time.

I raised my hand, no longer shaking, and, drinking deeply, I watched for Juan Luis to return alone.

THE PIER

Some tales we hear affect us, whether we wish them to or not. I choose to lend an ear because it is my calling to do so or, rather, it is such to listen and record and place events before you; but you should believe me when I say that I frequently wish I had not heard the tale at all – for where there is joy, there is often an equal measure of sorrow.

I heard one such tale when, upon my travels, I came across a small seaside town. It was positioned on the north eastern coast of an England already bitten by frosts and occasional snow, and at that time of winter when darkness fell so early you felt the day was over before it had rightly begun. Even so, the town endured with stoic resilience the winds that whipped across the bay, driving the grey sea into an occasional frenzy. Or at least, it seemed that way to me, as the beach huts, with peeling paint, stood stout against their elemental privations, and the rows of Victorian terraces, three stories high and but a pebble's throw from the shore, looked grim, but similarly determined not to quite fall into the ramshackle category – it was a close shave.

The population of the town was insignificant, perhaps by nature as well as by size; such was my unkind view, biased, perhaps, because I shivered beneath three layers and a camel duffel coat, unable to find even the least sign of a café, or a body to point me towards one. Hoisting my haversack higher upon my aching shoulders, I looked in vain for some respite, and at last, I sat down on a sand-worn bench near a stone wind-breaker facing that agitated sea. Hugging myself, I cursed my own wanderlust – a writer needs to feed himself and keep warm as much as the next man.

At last, I saw at a distance a figure walking towards me, slowly but with poise. It was a man, and as he drew near, I could see that he was dressed in a smart, black Alpaca greatcoat, his collar turned up high against the wind. He wore perfectly polished shoes and he held his Fedora hat on with one hand, gripping a walking stick with the other. His leather gloves – no doubt double-lined – kept his hands from freezing. As it was, he looked entirely out of place for 1968, even in such a place as this, which

9

Time itself seemed to have forgotten, or at least temporarily put aside.

I'm not sure if it was the wind that slowed his progress, or his gait, but it seemed to be an age before he was close enough for me to hail him; the cold was so biting that I think I would have grabbed him if he so much as walked a step past me without answering my greeting, which would quickly be followed by a plea for directions to somewhere I could stay or, at the least, obtain some hot food and drink. As it happened, he stopped forthwith and, with a slight twinkle, asked me if I was enjoying the weather. I took it in good spirit, and we both laughed.

"The centre of the town, such as it is, is that way," he spoke in a quite cultured voice, pointing away from the sea, "but you won't find much to cheer you there. If you want a bit of warmth and a good pint of mild, you had better come along with me." Saying this, he continued along the promenade.

I accepted with an inward shrug the snail's pace of travel, and we chatted as best we could above the sounds of the wind and the churning sea, until we approached a wooden pier. It was middling to long in size, and not only was it in a generally dilapidated condition, it looked as if it had been burnt, and the end, which would have stretched out into the waves, had collapsed. It was a sorry spectacle and, I thought, exactly in keeping with my impressions of the town. It piqued my interest nevertheless, as it looked as though it may once have had grander aspirations. I wondered how long it had been like this, and I resolved to ask my companion more about it.

We settled into a corner of a pub overlooking the bay and the pier nearby, and which was, although slightly seedy, surprisingly more cheerful than I had feared, with both evidence of refurbishment and an old-world charm. The landlord served me two pints of light mild, and when I asked my gentleman acquaintance – that is how I viewed him, for anyone who dressed in that manner could only be a gentleman – about the pub, he told me that it had been there for nearly 150 years.

"And the pier?" I enquired.

"Ah, now…" he looked at me sideways. "Ah, now…" he repeated. "It was originally built in 1910, that is, at the end of the golden age of pier building. It was later renovated into one of the last pleasure piers to be built in England."

I struggled to equate pleasure with either the town or the pier. Before I could ask him more, he swiftly steered the conversation to other things, and I discovered that he was a poet and an academic from Cambridge. He seemed delighted to discover that I was a literary soulmate.

"Oxbridge?" he asked.

"Durham University", I smiled.

"Ah well, can't be helped." But again, he said it with a twinkle in his eyes, so I could not possibly be offended.

Curiously, I could not draw him further on the pier, and after we had finished our drinks, I began to worry about where I might stay.

He looked at me and said, "It seems as though I'm fated to be your guardian. I stay at the Grey Gull Hotel when I'm here." He laughed somewhat wryly. "There are few other places now, but there are always vacancies. I visit here at this time every year. Is there a more melancholy place than a seaside town in winter? And yet I don't find it so! The quietude and the harsh weather act as muses for my poems. Humour, I enjoy...loneliness and tragedy are what drive my work."

These were unusual comments, yet I felt I understood what he meant when we vacated the pub and found a swiftly darkening sky above our heads and a solitary dog walker on the shingle and sand beach. My spirits drooped by the minute. We walked mostly in silence for about a quarter of a mile, before he stopped outside one of the Victorian terrace houses that lined the deserted road opposite the beach. Looking back, I could just see the black outline of the pier against a white moon that had, it seemed, arisen out of the sea itself this very minute. I forced my eyes away, and we entered the Grey Gull Hotel, which had a yellowing "Rooms Vacant" sign on the door, and which was, in effect, a bed and breakfast establishment – "hotel" was too grand a word for it.

A woman greeted us – if greet is the right expression. Rather sour-faced, she did not look bothered whether she had a new guest or not. However, she did smile slightly when she saw her regular guest and was slightly less disinterested, offering me a choice of rooms at varying prices; given my financial circumstances, as a less than famous author, I decided to take the cheapest, which turned out to be at the top of the house. The woman, herself, could have been aged anything between thirty and forty-five - she had that kind of face. Her hair, however, was almost entirely grey, which aged her considerably.

Whilst I was registering my particulars, my companion, who I now knew by name as Mr Blackwell, took off his hat, and, with a nod to me, went into the lounge. When I followed shortly afterwards, I found a room which had a drab, 1950s look about it, but which was surprisingly homely and warm; I sank into a plaid high back chair opposite Mr. Blackwell.

I looked around me and I could see that the guests were few. There was a woman of about 60 in a pale blue, long-sleeved dress wearing a string of faux pearls, reading by the window; a man of roughly the same age, smoking a pipe, and wearing a shirt and tie, but also, in a concession to the time of the evening, a grey cardigan instead of a jacket, with matching flannel trousers; and a young couple in the corner keeping to themselves and, I suspect, happy to do so.

At first, the conversation flowed along general lines between myself and Mr. Blackwell, then, as I had intended, I eventually raised, as a topic of discussion, the pier. At this, he looked slightly uneasy – there was no sign of his ready twinkle – and he looked around cautiously at the other guests as if fearing that they may overhear something of confidence.

I raised my eyebrows at Mr Blackwell, meaning to speak, but he silently put his right forefinger to his lips, and then merely rose from his chair, I presumed to retire to bed. He rested a hand lightly upon my shoulder as he passed me, murmuring, "Tomorrow…"

Can there be anything more galling to a writer? Until that moment, I had been only mildly interested in the history of the pier. But now, I found myself musing upon it while I sat alone, then again whilst I followed the colourless, taciturn landlady up three flights of stairs covered with a thin, olive carpet, and yet again as I undressed and shivered in a chilly, barely furnished attic overlooking the sea. I was determined to think that there could not be anything noteworthy about the pier or anything connected with it...in which case, why did I lie, unsleeping, for an hour or more, with an image of a structure, sharp and black against the sea, timbers askew, that may once have stretched proudly out above the waves but was now a sad relic? And why, when at last I fell asleep, did I dream of red and yellow flames rising above it, fierce and hot, encircling and entwining it until, defeated, it crumpled into steaming waters...?

I woke to sunshine flooding through an attic window without curtains – one gets very little for the money I paid – which dispelled any remnants of gloom. The rays could not oust the chill from the air, however, so I quickly shaved and washed in order to get downstairs, where I was hopeful of getting some warmth. As I shaved, I saw in the mirror a man of nearly thirty, hair long and dark and with that slightly peeved look in his eyes that said, as if I did not already know, he had still not achieved, in the literary world, all that he knew himself to be capable of – which was surely more than a few (although fairly well-received) articles and stories here and there and an unfinished novel mouldering in a drawer. Sighing, I went down to breakfast.

The other guests had not yet risen, and I found Mr Blackwell sitting alone, as if waiting for me, and after greeting me, he said softly, "Let us go for a walk. . . no, no, do eat first, of course. . ." I ordered some tea from the landlady, who, in her silent, gloomy fashion, poured it from a white china pot. Having drunk quickly, I munched on some toast and marmalade as we made our way out onto the promenade into white sunshine that sparkled on the waters of a cold, blue sea.

We turned left, walking on in silence. The path turned left again and steeped upwards, and after a few minutes, we reached a greensward on the top of a hill, where benches were set, overlooking the promenade and the sea. The wind was still cold, despite the sun, and as we sat, I pulled my coat tightly around me. All was silent apart from the sighing of the wind and the murmur of the waves some distance away; the tide was out, and the beach, such as it was, had become a vast mud flat.

"You can see the pier clearly from here," commented Mr Blackwell, and indeed we could, as it leaned outward, crooked and broken. I could see that without the waters below, it was some height above the ugly mud. "You were curious about the pier and so I shall tell you of it, as it was told to me by those remaining locals who know."

Mr Blackwell wrapped his woollen scarf tightly around his neck and chin; when he spoke, his voice was occasionally muffled, but I shall always remember every word I heard.

"This town is small, but it was smaller still as little as fifteen years ago. The pub was here before the Victorian terraces, and the terraces were here before the town centre, and the town centre, small as it is, was here before the pier." He paused. "It was a quiet place, and in its time, the only visitors were from Hull, who would come for the day to breathe in the sea air. But district councillors, being what they are, had aspirations for the town. The pier had been a genteel construction when George V ascended the throne, and throughout the two world wars, but when our current Majesty was crowned, things went a little wild."

Smiling wryly, he continued, "They decided to make the pier the main attraction, the beacon that would attract visitors; expansion, tourism...money." He nodded slowly. "So they extended the pier, taking it right out among the waves, installed two penny arcades, some children's rides, a café right at the end... it shocked the locals, who were used to a peaceful life, but some saw it as an opportunity, and these very terrace houses above which we sit...well, at least some of them became *hotels*, as the owners like to call them."

He sighed a little as he said, "Not my kind of thing at all, I'm afraid, but I did not begin coming here until after... well, let me carry on." Shivering in the wind, he continued, "One couple who set up a B & B had two daughters. The second one was unexpected, so by the time she was born, there were 10 years between the two...but she certainly couldn't have been loved more, particularly by her older sister. As for the younger, Helen, she followed the elder, Catherine, wherever she went – there couldn't be a more mutual adoration – that is, until the pier attracted something they hadn't encountered before."

"Oh?"

"Why, boys of course! Or I would call them men, or near enough. Catherine was 17 then, and after a short lifetime of ennui, if not boredom, an influx of moody teenagers in black leather jackets and hair swept back was a welcome excitement. Some of them were actually reasonable looking – or at least one of them was, because when he began paying attention to Catherine, she couldn't help but feel flattered. I don't say he was a bad youth...he was just that, a youth."

He said this simply, as if that explained everything – and perhaps it did. What else is there to say when girls and boys become men and women?

"Of course, her mother and father were protective of her, but they couldn't keep her locked up. Catherine went out as often as she could, but Helen wanted to go along too, and her parents were sanguine about this...seeing her, as it were, as almost a mini-chaperone." Mr Blackwell smiled in a grim fashion. "It was quite a good ploy, to begin with, at least. They would meet at the pier, play in the arcades, and drink and eat innocently at the café looking out towards the North Sea...pretty bleak, I would say, but Catherine couldn't be happier – this was growing up, this was romance of a kind! Except, of course, the lad wanted more..."

I said nothing, just nodding once or twice. I wondered why he was telling me these things but, almost instantly, I realised that it was because he recognised in me a kindred literary spirit, with a curiosity about life, and in much the same way that he would have heard the tale he was willing to pass it on to me. When he mentioned boys, I thought that I knew where this was leading...the same old story. But I was wrong, and later, I wished it had merely been the case.

"It was at the very end of autumn, with a hint of the impending winter in the air, when the boy told Catherine that he loved her - whether he really did or not is neither here nor there. The fact is that she believed him – and they had not even kissed yet! Such was her naiveté...but she wanted him to kiss her at least, and what better place was there than at the end of the pier, with the sound of the wind and the sea egging on her romantic thoughts. Of course, it might have turned out to be just a sneaked kiss, or more likely, a fumble behind the café..."

I tried to remember what I was like as a much younger man, but I couldn't exactly recall how such a small intrigue would have felt – I guess university allowed more opportunity for fraternising than such snatched liaisons.

"By all accounts, it was a Sunday afternoon, and although it was not late, the sun seemed already quite low in the sky above the town when she decided to leave her house." Mr Blackwell pulled his scarf tighter around him as a cloud passed theatrically across the sun. "And of course, her sister wanted to go too, as always, but for once, Catherine did not want this. She asked her to stay at home but frustratingly for her, her parents insisted she took her along – I suspect they felt something was in the offing and wanted to head it off. It was perhaps...no, most definitely, selfish of them...they were, in effect, passing on their own responsibility to a mere child." He shook his head. "I've often wondered what possessed them... it was a foolishness that they came to regret bitterly."

For the first time, I began to wish I was not listening to this story – I felt a prickly feeling at the base of my neck and a tingle along my temples. I murmured to myself, and Mr Blackwell, as if I had spoken to him, replied, "Eh? Negligent? Yes," he said slowly, "yes, perhaps it was. . ." Shaking his head once more, he continued.

"It wasn't the best of times for an assignation. It had begun to rain, and the winds were high and threatening. Catherine was worried that the boy would not be there. I can imagine that as she hurried along, her heart beating hard against her chest, she held an underlying resentment that her sister – the sister who loved her with a deep and trusting love – was beside her, scurrying to keep up on her little legs, and who, in her innocence, would have failed to understand why the person she loved more than any other was irritated with her – almost angry - and did not want her there."

I did not turn my head when I heard something that could have been a swallow – surely not a sob? – from this educated man, who, though not worldly-wise, knew enough of romance and tragedy from the poetry of the ages to be so affected by the thought of a love felt by a vulnerable being towards one she trusted, and from whom she sought nothing but love in return. I merely looked straight towards the pier, clenched my jaw and blinked as the cold wind stung my eyes, making them water – I believe it was the wind – when he told me that the young couple met as they had agreed, that they hurried to the end of the pier -

now assailed with a rancorous squall with white spray reaching almost to the rails – that, just as Catherine raised her face to be kissed, her little sister tugged at her skirt, and she shouted at her in passion, *'For goodness sake Helen, GO AWAY!'* She heard her gasp and run, and when that kiss – that blighted kiss – was still but incomplete, there was a scream...and the little one was gone."

The blood left my face. When I finally looked at Mr Blackwell again, he said, "The rails on the pier were not particularly well designed, you see. They had wide spaces between them, and loose rivets made worse by frequent storms...This coupled with a platform of slickened wooden slats to walk on and the violent winds that afternoon... well...it was a freak accident, of course, and you may argue it could have happened at any time and to any unfortunate person...but it didn't."

"God..."

He said firmly, "There was no God present. It was high tide, and she was not found until the waves receded the following day. She was there, on the mud flats, if not directly below the pier, at least within sight of it."

Mr Blackwell stood, and we began to walk slowly down the hill in silence. Finally, as we approached the hotel, I reflected aloud: "It's almost too much to bear."

"It was. It acted like a drug on the town. Soon, the parents and Catherine left. Even if the parents forgave her, they could never forgive themselves. As for Catherine she drove herself almost senseless with remorse. Any exuberance the town may have had simply drained away, just like the people in it, and it is now as you find it."

We made our way carefully up the steps of the Grey Gull Hotel, where I hoped to find some warmth, and perhaps peace of mind, once more.

Pausing at the stained and cracked ochre door, he said, "Of course, it did not help that the pier burnt down two days after the tragedy."

I stopped and looked at him.

"What happened to Catherine?" I asked quietly.

He pushed the door open. "Oh...she came back...eventually."

We entered the lounge and sat in two of the high back chairs in front of the fire. Picking up a small bell that sat on an oval, chestnut coffee table, he shook it, so that its chimes rang throughout the still room and echoed into the hallway. The landlady appeared noiselessly, and Mr Blackwell watched me as he spoke to her gently.

"Catherine, could we have a pot of tea please?"

The landlady merely nodded, looking from me to Mr Blackwell and back again, while I tightened my jaws fearing they would fall open. And then I wondered how I could have missed that look in her eyes – unending anguish, buried deep within her but barely contained, and I realised she had returned to punish herself perpetually by living within sight of the pier, which was only of wood and steel but represented death…and a little girl's broken heart.

I took up my cup with a shaking hand, and I decided that if I had been she, I would have burned down the pier too.

THE GENTLEMEN'S CLUB

One of the enduring niceties of the Dionysius club was that it overlooked Pall Mall. As a consequence, the seats beneath those famous oak-timbered and multi-paned bay windows were much in demand by those members of a curious turn of mind – that is if they could rouse themselves from their port-induced torpor – and if they wished to observe the comings and goings of early 20th century London. If truth be known, the indolence of the members, mostly of the lower aristocracy with a smattering of nobler peers of the realm, was not breached often enough for them to display any great excitement at outside activity unless it interfered with their own way of life.

Notwithstanding, the Lords Arthur Basley and Henry Carmichael, Earls both, were frequently to be seen at their ease smoking a cigar or two as they commented offhandedly upon those they observed. If they could be bothered to raise a sneer, occasionally they did.

It was while standing at those same bay windows that the noble Lords first set eyes upon Harry Clarke as he lowered himself heavily from a hackney carriage, the four horses blowing somewhat with the strain. Lord Basley noted that the portly passenger, who was unknown to them, was free enough with his money and the cabbie gave a nod and a cheery wave as he urged the horses on their way. The man, fedora-hatted and wearing a loud Prince-of-Wales check overcoat on a warmer than average October afternoon – causing him to perspire even more than the horses – stood in slightly bemused fashion below them until a figure they knew well bounded down the marble steps and held out his hand whilst grinning. Then, having greeted each other warmly, they both entered the foyer and disappeared from view.

'Well…' drawled Lord Basley.

'What on earth does Camford mean by bringing him inside?' said the other.

They looked at each other and blew smoke rings in a lazy fashion before Basley shrugged and commented on the fact that His Grace, the Duke of Camford, did not have the decorum or deference that his recently deceased father, former president of the Dionysius, had always displayed. Sinking easily into their green, now rather shabby, leather Chesterfields, they picked up late editions of *The Times* to familiarise themselves with the happenings of the day and put His Grace and his unusual guest out of their minds.

It was to be expected in the gallery room that most members, who retired here after some heavy-duty eating, would be able to read (if enough energy could be generated) or indulge in a post-prandial snooze without interruption. The Tea Room, in reality, the dining room, always provided – via the most deferential and liveried waiters one could imagine – a fairly sumptuous lunch (although it had been remarked upon recently that standards had been dropping) followed by a cheese smorgasbord and port; this usually set the members up for immobility.

This being so, and expecting nothing to disturb this idleness, it was a surprise to the dozen or so who sat quietly at their ease to find their somnolence sorely interrupted when the Duke strolled in accompanied by his so-recently-discussed companion, and began to introduce him in a quiet fashion to various members of the establishment. If any of these were of an observant or curious nature it might have been noted that His Grace had a slight air of excitement about him alongside his genuine pleasure at the discomfiture of a number of the more condescending members.

Camford espied the two seated Earls and ushered his guest in their direction. Their Lordships looked at each other meaningfully as the pair approached, one of them slim and tall in a fashionable navy double-breasted suit, and the other in a maroon three-piece tailored for someone of a somewhat lesser bulk. As they drew near it could be seen that, in fact, the attire of both was equally well tailored and they wore crisp white shirts with wing-tip collars and ties and Oxford brogue shoes – although the Earls seriously doubted that the more rotund of the two had been within 60 miles of Oxford. Both the Earls, however, privately acknowledged that he at least was monied – the phrase 'where there's muck there's brass' occurred to both, although they could not have said where they had heard the expression.

Neither man rose immediately from their seats when the Duke introduced them to Mr Harvey Clarke; it was the act of two patronising aristocrats and certainly not that of gentlemen but eventually they both stood and rather limply shook hands and when Basley, in his lazy way, said (not meaning it of course) that he was delighted to meet Mr Clarke, the response came back briskly and jovially in a West Yorkshire accent.

'Eh, Harry's good enough for me your Lordship. We don't stand on ceremony where I come from you know.'

Basley raised an eyebrow, 'I'm afraid we do in these parts Mr Clarke.'

The bluff Yorkshireman laughed, 'As you wish Your Lordship, as you wish – each man to his own, eh?'

The Duke chuckled, 'You'll find no airs about Harry, Basley. It was so when I escorted his daughter to the Oxford commemoration ball. Delightful young lady.'

'Ay that's so Your Grace, she's good enough for any man.'

'I'm sure,' the Earl replied coldly. He reappraised the commoner and recognised that although Mr Clarke might not have been to University himself, he had enough clout and finance to ensure that his daughter certainly did.

Lord Carmichael spoke, 'And what brings you down to London, Mr Clarke?'

'A bit of business, sir,' he said with the hint of a twinkle in his eye, and again the Duke chuckled, which set Basley on edge and made him irritable as Carmichael merely asked what line of work Mr Clarke was in.

'Oh, buying, selling, whatever turns a profit, My Lord. Made my first million in tea, my second in spirits, and my third…well, I'm not quite there yet but I'm branching out sir, branching out!' he beamed.

The Earls resumed their seats and Basley took up his newspaper with a mutter, 'So pleased to meet you Mr Clarke.'

The Duke and his guest merely looked at each other and shrugged, and then the former winked and nodded towards the Tea Room, 'Let's get you a bite to eat Harry, that is if our noble Lords have not snaffled the last of the cheese.'

As they turned away, Basley leaned towards Carmichael and spoke deliberately in a voice just loud enough to be heard by the Duke and his guest, which caused them both to stop dead.

'A tradesman, Carmichael...'

Basley's friend was just decent enough to look a little abashed and muttered, 'Well, hardly that Basley...a merchant...'

'Merchant, tradesman...such little difference to my mind. This is a gentlemen's club...' and he raised his voice once again and said firmly, 'Money does not make a gentleman.'

With the Duke's good humour vanishing as swiftly as the tea room cheese, he moved to remonstrate but was held by a light touch on his arm; Harry shook his head slightly and continued to beam his widest of smiles. The Duke shrugged once more and reluctantly he was steered towards the door by the businessman. In his anger, the Duke did not notice that above that smile there was a curious glint in the eyes of Mr Harvey Clarke.

*

Becoming a member of the Dionysius Club was a straightforward affair but curiously humiliating for those candidates who were rejected. In line with the majority of private clubs, it involved 'blackballing' whereby a candidate is voted upon by current members in a secret ballot using white and black balls; at the Dionysius, it took only two black balls in the ballot box to heap humiliation upon the poor prospective member. Naturally, reactions differed depending on their character: the true gentlemen, the type who would, in fact, have been an asset to the club, laughed it off, others would take umbrage, sometimes publicly, and vow that they never really wanted to be a member in the first place. Yet more would merely smile (while secretly slighted) and consider how best they might take their revenge – the difficulty being of course that they never knew for sure who had voted against them (though suspicions abounded) and teeth were gnashed accordingly.

By contrast, elections of a current member to the presidency were an open affair and a majority would see the candidate through; in this way, the Duke of Camford took up the position quite comfortably. This was in part because of the virtues of his recently deceased father, who was well respected, and many feeling (perhaps incorrectly) that these same virtues would surely manifest themselves in the son. In addition, the younger members, though few, were fully on his side and believed (rightly as it happens) that a breath of fresh air should blow through these fusty rooms, which were looking increasingly shabby; if truth be known both the club and its members needed a good sprucing.

Mr Harvey Clarke's application for membership was rejected at the next quarterly ballot. It being December, one would have hoped that there was an element of seasonal goodwill but six of the 60 balls in the ballot box were black, and although Harry appeared to take this in good spirit, the Duke and the other young bucks who had nominated him were put out and muttered amongst themselves. His Grace had a pretty accurate idea of who the naysayers were and sent the odd glower in their direction as he strode into the gallery room; he saved the darkest for the Lords Basley and Carmichael who sat, smiling smugly, beneath the window smoking their pipes and imbibing their port.

There was something infuriating to the Duke as he looked across at the two, Carmichael, stout, white-haired and pompous, and Basley, thin, yet still self-indulgent, with a widow's peak of black hair above glittering eyes and a patrician nose. The Duke spoke of them to Harry later that evening in his city apartments who only smiled and asked who else he believed had voted against his admission. When the Duke named others of the more elderly and longstanding members, obdurate in their opposition to change, Harry merely nodded and smiled once more before offering the Duke a snifter of his finest brandy, imported by himself, of course.

*

In March, as spring peeped its head around the seasonal corner, only two black balls stymied Harry's second pitch at being admitted. The Duke was always nonplussed at Harry's calm demeanour when things did not go his way but apart from the obvious fact that one was an aristocrat who had throughout his life been given things on a silver platter, and the other a self-made millionaire (richer than most of the cosseted members of the Dionysius), they differed in character as much as the proverbial chalk and cheese. This did not impede their unlikely friendship, which was based around the Duke's growing affection for Harry's charming daughter - and their appreciation of life's absurdities. Unlike Harry, however, the Duke, who was genial but mercurial, age yet to play a part in tempering this facet of his nature, could not help but agitate when he and the witnesses emptied the box and saw, stark against the white, those ebony spheres of rejection.

Harry, on the other hand, who was of the driven but steadiest Yorkshire type, simply shrugged his shoulders and continued with his daily business, making frequent appearances at the club as the Duke's guest; it was noted by Basley and Carmichael that many members now spoke with Harry quite readily. Carmichael's curiosity was piqued but Basley was merely exasperated; it did not occur to him that there was more to being a gentleman than nobility, that courtesy, a generous spirit, and open-mindedness were characteristics of greater importance.

*

The summer heat in June was of the kind that made most people tetchy; this certainly included members of the Dionysius as they sat attempting to keep cool in the gallery room. *The Times* was of more use as a fan or as a face-covering for those fitfully snoozing in their armchairs than as a source of world, business, or financial news. As it happened, if many had paid greater attention in the past to such matters, particularly those of a financial nature, their own circumstances on large estates, grandiose in name and title, would not be – as it was in some cases – quite so dire; the upkeep of the landed gentry was a costly affair.

Lords Basley and Carmichael were in their customary leather chairs. The former, who was waxing wroth about the state of the club, its food, décor, and general deterioration as an establishment for gentlemen, did not notice that his companion was rather on the quiet side.

'I say,' said an extravagantly dressed young toff to another as they passed nearby, 'have you heard the news? Harry has been voted in.'

'Hip, hip!' said the other as they proceeded upon their way, 'let's go and have a snifter!'

Basley slowly withdrew the pipe he was about to light from between his lips and stared at Carmichael, a stare that would have frozen all parts of a brass monkey regardless of the weather outside.

'What…?' he began.

But Carmichael's nerve broke and he babbled, 'I…well…it's just that…oh damn it! College fees are so expensive for the boys, and the old estate needs a jolly good going over, that chandelier in the grand hall needs replacing, and…' he trailed off.

Lord Basley seethed in silence but made his feelings known with the clenching of his teeth on the empty pipe, which he had now replaced in his mouth for that sole purpose. It was a betrayal, there was no doubt of that, and he could imagine that as they emptied the ballot box last night how sadly rebellious his solitary black ball would have looked amongst the pristine white of the others, and how there would have been knowing looks as to its owner amongst the expressions of satisfaction; he felt bitter indeed – the name 'Judas' came to his lips but he held his tongue.

'Morning milords, a fine day though happen a bit hot for some.' Harry stood beside them beaming and rubbing his hands; the Duke was at his side trying not to grin.

Lord Basley was not quite beaten, he stood and said, 'I believe congratulations are in order Mr Clarke, although…'

'Oh please, milord,' interrupted Harry, 'let's have no more of the 'Mr Clarke', call me Harry do. We're all gentlemen here,' His eyes twinkled.

Lord Basley's eyes narrowed, 'I've said it before Mr Clarke – money does not make a gentleman.'

At this Mr Harvard Clarke puffed out his chest, 'That's so sir, I'd not deny it – but it certainly talks Your Lordship, it certainly talks.' And he gave Lord Basley his best Yorkshire wink.

SILKS

There now, ain't it the truth! Talk about turns – do a good 'un and it comes right back on you. I'm too soft, me, Charley always says so, an' 'e's a mate o' mine. Good with 'is 'ands, 'e is – well, usually, like, - but 'e's slipped up good and proper now and the new lad's been nabbed! It's Newgate or the colonies for the lot of us if 'e squawks! An' all for a silk. Some'll say it was me wot made a pig's ear of it, but it was Charley, I'm setting the record straight.

Gawd knows wot 'im I calls "my old genelman" will say when 'e finds out, 'cos it will likely mean 'im swingin' nice and quiet at last with 'is feet off the floor – and the rope won't even be of quality, you can count on it. That's the trouble, see, 'e's always told us to go for quality:

"Boys," 'e says, *"Boys, its quality I'm after. Gold... luvverly. A nice timepiece... perfick. Silk 'andkerchief... can't beat it, bring it 'ome."* So, when we sees a toff blowing 'is 'onk wiv a beautiful red silk, spotted all over with silver flowers, I gives Charley a nudge and a nod and says to the new 'un to keep close and watch an expert at work, so to speak. I can see he 'ain't 'appy though and I'm beginning to wish I 'adn't set eyes on 'im then.

I first sees 'im in Barnet town a-looking oh so sorry for 'imself an' 'ungry to boot but I got an 'eart (some sez!) an' after passing 'im on the step a few times I goes over and says: *"'Ello, me covey, what's the row?"*

Sure enough: *"'Ungry and tired,"* 'e says, an' *"seven days on the road,"* and blow me if 'e don't look to start blubbing so I rather 'asty, like, tells 'im I'll stump up, and off we go to bag some 'am and a fourpenny bran afore 'e starves to death. We takes it alongside a pot of beer in the public 'ouse and 'e wolfs it down, all the while lookin' at me - I s'pose 'e can't be more than twelve years an' probably ain't used to seeing a fine young gent like meself. 'E's a tad taller than me, I'd say, but not so well dressed for sure though I'll grant you me trousers is loose and trail a bit and I 'ave to keep me sleeves rolled up to keep me 'ands free – but that's an advantage in my line of work anyways! 'E ain't got no 'at either.

'As 'e got any lodgings or money? Not a bit of it, so I says to 'im 'e's coming along wiv me to London where my old genelman will look after 'im like 'e does me – at which point I can see 'im lookin' me up and down, doubtful, like, wiv them wide eyes. I could take offence but off we go and we reach Islington turnpike just afore the clocks are striking eleven of the hour – which suited me 'cos as a general rule I prefer the dark when makin' me way 'ome.

When we gets to Saffron 'Ill, and me lodgings alongside Field Lane, I takes 'im up to meet the lads an' my genelman, who was so pleased to meet his acquaintance, 'e welcomes 'im proper wiv some more grub and an 'ot gin and water. I can see 'e's never seen so many silks – just 'anging on the clothes-'orse they were, dryin' – but we puts 'im to bed as 'e's all-in.

Well, the next few days, we play this game, see? The new 'un is told to try and take these wipes out of me ol' genelman's pocket wivout 'im knowing. What a lark! 'E's got no idea!

This mornin' 'e's told 'e's got to earn 'is keep, like. O' course, I 'ad told 'im to consider 'imself one of the family but we all got to make a livin', ain't we? So, me old genelman packs us all off and says: *"Be back soon, boys,"* though I know 'e means by that *"Don't come back unless you got something to show for it."* I can tell the new 'un ain't got a clue what 'es got to do but 'e'll know soon enough and when 'e does I won't 'ave 'im putting on airs wiv me – not when I've got an 'at like mine and 'e ain't got one at all.

Well, 'ere we are now in a fix! 'Cos Charley cods it up and when the toff feels 'is 'andkerchief movin' in a direction contrary to 'is pocket or 'is nose 'e turns round and sees the new 'un, who, now the penny 'as dropped, is off like a whippet. All credit to 'im, 'e's fast for a skinny 'un, but 'e don't know 'is way round, see? So, me and Charley, we joins in the hullabaloo, givin' the occasional shout of *"Stop, thief!"* so we don't seem out of place in the crowd and, sure enough, 'e's nabbed as you might expect and Gawd knows but that 'e'll squawk alright.

It's off 'ome now for us to break it to the ol' genelman an' 'e ain't going to like it - but 'e çan't do without us, oh no! Where will 'e get 'is silver and 'is gold and 'is chains an' 'is wallets from then, eh? So, we'll pack it all up, silks an' all, and I can tell you we'll be changing lodgings quick, like, or my name ain't the Artful Dodger!'

27

AS I SAILED, AS I SAILED

Oh, blow once more for me, blusterous wind, for tomorrow I hang by the neck!

If Newgate's walls constrain my flesh, they cannot bind my soul. This night I will stand again at bow of ship and gaze upon timeless seas; in grand spirit I will sail swiftly on buoyant waves. I will hear the clash of sword and harsh voices laugh and curse, and I will gander at the moon. For I sailed with Captain Kidd, and if this acquaintance has brought me down it is one that I do not regret; it raised me up before this doom.

A man of letters I once was and by the good offices of chaplain and gentleman – the rarest of things within these prison walls – I use this quill to lay down my tale, in the year of our King William, 1701, that you may know what man Kidd was. Yes, for certain piratical, possessed of violence, and masterful, though not always master of himself. And yet...I was present when he bid Mrs. Raymond hold out her apron and filled it with gold for hospitality she had shown, and when the Trinity Church of New York City gave thanks for his aid in its construction; and if the governor of such a province calls a man "trusty and well beloved" you may believe there is more worthy substance to him than that of greed.

Of which, if it is greed that obliges your reading and it is Kidd's treasure you seek...well, if such a revelation transpires herein it is of no moment to me; the truest treasure may be in the knowing of the man.

You may think that New York is of import and you are not wrong, for in that city my captain had friends in authority, though not always of loyal persuasion, and he married the widow Sarah Bradley in '91. Some doubt the veracity of his love, she being of substantial inherited wealth, but I give assurance of their mutual devotion and Kidd was one for making his own way in the world. Could the poor son of a long-dead Dundee minister be anything other than firm of purpose when he traverses the seas and there is violence and betrayal at every turn? You shall know to what I refer.

It was in New York that I met Kidd and found he took a liking to me as much as I admired him; as it was, he had already made his name as a great privateer and, further, defended the island of Nevis against the French. The *Blessed William* was his vessel of renown (until she was stolen in Antigua by the blackguard pirate Culliford, curse his name).

I will avow that in his original endeavours he was steadfast and loyal to King, England and her colonies. The line between privateer and pirate being of vague distinction, he was not the first to cross it, neither will he be the last, yet the one is praised whilst the other is punishable by death; and when our Crown enjoins the former to "take their pay from the French" is it wonder that pillage is rife, and hungry crews of violent bent are held solely in check through will of the captain in charge? When needs must, such masters will let them have their head; in the year of our meeting alone the *Blessed William* had sacked the island of Marie-Galante, clearing two thousand pounds in gold and, in the defence of New England, enemy privateers, rich in lucre, were boarded and violence served upon them.

I was but a young and sleepy clerk in the residences of the Earl of Bellomont, duly appointed Governor of New York, Massachusetts and New Hampshire, yet I came full awake on the morning of William Kidd's arrival. He was of the middling height but appeared taller, for though not periwigged his hair was long to shoulder, and curled, and stood high on his head. It was black, as were his breeches, whilst his stockings, which showed off a fine turn of leg, and his coat were of the bloodiest red; he wore also a gold linen band about the waist. I recall that there were white frills at sleeve and neck – but it is by black, red and gold that I will remember him best. I know now that by design he had found these had the greatest effect in his official dealings; when he appraised those in authority with his dark eye, and oft time similar countenance, there were not many that would gainsay him, yet when the mood took him his laugh displayed a warmer spirit. When he nodded at me, he looked thoughtful, though I knew not why at that time.

Bellomont and the captain were well acquainted in that the first had propositioned the second with ridding the seas of Thomas Tew, famed as the Rhode Island pirate, and all associates thereof. In truth, this was not a proposition to bear refusal, coming as it did with *Letters of Marque* direct from His Majesty, enjoining Kidd also to attack French vessels with impunity. My thoughts were that this commission would be taken up with ardour, and so it was.

When the pair had concluded their discussions, of which I was not party despite earnest endeavours and my ear to the door, Bellomont strolled from his study with Kidd, picked up his stick and the two made to leave. It was at that moment the captain, firstly with words to the governor, who, in his portliness, made Kidd look yet taller still, and then with those direct to me, diverted me from that clerical path I had been set upon by a well-meaning father. I did not know so but worlds were to change!

"Come lad," I recall that his voice was quiet yet brim with authority, "to the harbour and you shall see a ship worthy of the name *Adventure.*"

I looked to Bellomont, who gave the curtest of nods and the tightest of smiles at which I swiftly gathered my hat and followed in their wake.

If my desk and daily labour constrained me physically with its swamp of dockets and papers and depositions it was the harbour that lifted my spirit whenever it came to mind – which was often. And so it was that day; the wharf was the creaking hulls of ships and rattling masts, the cries of hungry gulls, the smell of sea and salt, the loading and unloading of wares and the compounding of mariners and of gentlemen come to inspect and express their ownerships. Standing proud above the clamour was the *Adventure Galley.*

It was at that moment I, Hugh Lamley, barely seventeen in years, slight in body and of perpetually roving mind, did become resolute; I would match desire with deeds and throw down my quill. Like a bird from which such feathers came I would be served by the wind, and borne to places afar, and though I had but just then determined this in my heart, Kidd looked down upon me with the merest of knowing smiles.

I listened in earnest to the conversation of the two principals as they admired the ship. She weighed middling-large at 284 tons burthen, and was sail-rigged with three masts, but was furnished un-common with two banks of oars giving the advantage in calm weather over other ships dead in the water. She was a ship built for war; equipped for thirty-four cannon and 150 men and though she had sailed from England short-handed - yet still taking a French vessel as prize on the way - Kidd assured the governor he would take pride in selecting both officers and crew himself for a full complement before they sailed five weeks hence.

Oh, did my ears ring and my eyes shine! My very wish was that I should be aboard this ship, Father notwithstanding. I will not tire you with the strains accrued during my adjurations to that beloved man, for I preferred his blessing; my resolve wavered but once, when he sat with head bowed and the greying of his hair stood stark to my eyes, yet when he raised himself he looked me in the eye, clasped me firmly by the hand and nodded and whispered my name. My eyes did blur but my grip for once was equal to the task, for I felt that I was a man at last...

And so it was I stepped on deck; by the solicitous accommodation of the captain, who had begun in much the same way, I was a seaman's apprentice. The month was September, the year, 1696, and we were steering for India upon deep seas.

Of the crew, there were two aboard who were profound in their effect upon me, and for the mortal consequences of our voyage. By their different characters was there exemplified the hidden unease with which we sailed; as I later found, Kidd had been unable to engage men to his own standards and fully half the crew were, or had been, pirates or cut-throats or, more likely, both.

The quartermaster, Hendrick, was a man of Dutch persuasion, yet with skin so swarthy as to be almost black; despite his ugliness he was a man of fair nature unless disturbed. He was loyal to Kidd, who entrusted him with instructing me in the use of the cutlass and flintlock when his time permitted. With cutlass, being of the same small build as myself, he taught me well how to use my speed to best advantage and seemed pleased at my progress, and I had a good eye with the pistol; on occasion he shared with me, too, tales of the sea, which he loved as much as I did.

The second was William Moore. Though it was the quartermaster who ought speak for the crew, Moore took it upon himself to speak for those of them who were forever dissatisfied;

31

his black-bearded countenance was ideal for this purpose for it never seemed to be anything other than surly. I felt that there were bad deeds behind him and in front. I did not like him, nor he, I.

I had little time to dwell on thoughts such as these in the months ahead for my duties made me cabin boy and swabbie and even powder monkey at varying times and combined to exhaust me; yet many of the crew were of the opinion that I was bonded to the sea from the start, as I was sure-footed and swayed to the rhythm of the waves and suffered not from the sickness that accompanied those first at sea.

Not once did I crave the shore, but I was reminded at times that our purpose was not admiration of the oceans when I heard the mutinous mutterings of the crew, Moore in particular; we had been under sail for half of a year and put in at Madeira, and the Verdes, and had rounded the Cape of Good Hope, at last, with but two failed attacks on French ships and very little lucre from several small traders to show for those arduous months at sea.

During one of these boardings I saved the captain's life. At the same time, I beheld both his fury and his mercy. We had taken the ship, *Mary,* with no loss of life on either side and Kidd, being of gentlemanly persuasion, took her captain, Parker, to his own cabin for private conversation. To his consternation, upon return to Parker's ship – now our own - he found that a certain portion of our crew had ransacked it. Kidd's outrage was something to behold. His face was as flint and there was behind his eye a murderous intent; though he did not raise his voice he commanded the booty to be returned. He stood with legs astride, his right hand rested lightly on the hilt of his cutlass and he faced down a surly gang, Moore among them. It was not he that made to attack the captain from behind but one of his cronies and I shouted a warning just in time. With swiftness and calm Kidd caught hold of the man, a red-headed salt with colour face to match, and threw him bodily to the floor; if Hendrick had not stayed his hand it is certain that he would have run the man through. In fairness, it would have been no more than he deserved, for his act was a mutinous one. As it was, the captain had him hauled off in chains and at last he roared his displeasure; with shame, the crew piled high the loot on the deck of the *Mary.*

After speech with Hendrick, Kidd showed great leniency and had the red-headed man merely hung up and drubbed with the flat of a cutlass. There was not a man among the crew who could argue with this, for they knew certain that mutiny was punishable by death. And it was an unintended death that sealed the captain's own fate, along with my own and others of loyalty to him; that, and a piratical act of great daring, though as I will now tell, a reluctant one.

We made sail to Madagascar and thence to the Comoros. I had feeling for the crew and myself at that time, for not only did we lose a vast number with the cholera at that place, with which I almost succumbed, but we had gained little booty. The ship herself was showing signs of wear, and I could see that this troubled the captain, and most likely made unhelpful contribution to his state of mind - and to the unwise act of braining William Moore!

A Dutch ship being hailed nearby, Moore and others urged the captain to attack her and would not take nay for answer. This being an outright act of piracy and, furthermore, certain to anger our Dutch born Majesty, Kidd refused. Harsh words were spoken and I watched as his anger, always quick, came to the boil. When he called Moore a "lousy dog", Moore replied: "If I am then you have made me so, and many more beside."

The captain roared and snatched up an iron pail at hand and hurled it forthwith at the head of Moore, who went down as solid and heavy as an anchor. We went silent, and Kidd bade him carried to the surgeon; he was dead the next day.

In my heart, although the captain seemed unconcerned at the consequence of his action, it is my belief this played upon his mind and we hunted like sharks, ever more desperate for cause to justify our endless roaming. In the new year, 1698, on the Malabar Coast we espied two merchantmen travelling under French colours and attacked. With accomplishment we took them both, the *Rouparelle* and the *Quedagh Merchant*, this last of 400 tons burthen or thereabouts, and though the resistance was brief, with flintlock I killed my first man. I had grown, my sinews were strong and I had been at sea for near two years, but for the first and only time I was sick.

What treasure abounded on the *Quedagh*! Gold, silver, satins, muslins and silks; there were enough of these to make even my meagre share considerable and the crew for once ceased their scowling and mutterings – until the captain found that the ship was running these goods for the English East India Company. Unless the goods were returned, this was piracy, undoubted.

I could see the indecision that for once shook Kidd; he was of loyal persuasion but I believe him worn down by the perpetual prospect of mutiny. The anger of the crew in this case would not be denied; even Hendrick was at one with them, and we voted to keep the treasure. We were now pirates!

From that point onward the winds of death were in our sails. The captain was sure that Bellomont would assist when he returned to New York; knowing the governor as I did, I was not of the same mind, yet, of a strangeness I felt no fear as we headed towards an unwelcome fate. I would not abandon my captain whatsoever, but there were others I knew would do so.

We crewed the three ships to the island of Sainte-Marie, which was a haven, if any place in these wild seas was, for pirates, smugglers, cut-throats and rogues, and we scuttled the *Adventure Galley*. I was not sorry to see her go down. She was the first ship in which I sailed, and she had at first beguiled me with her rugged beauty yet, truth be told, she had become worm-eaten and leaky; I feared that many of the crew were as afflicted as the ship. When we ran across Culliford, he who had stolen the *Blessed William*, I knew then that this was so, for the vastest number of the crew deserted to him; they were of a mind that they were sailing to certain death with Kidd, and furthermore that Culliford might provide them with richer pickings.

To me, it was sign of the captain's resigned spirit that, though in high dudgeon, he made no attempt to prevent the actions of this scurvy crew or take reprisal on a fellow captain who had twice played him false. Instead, Kidd renamed the *Quedagh* as the *Adventure Prize* and, with just thirteen hands, we weighed anchor.

Now, ye who read, I must come swift to the resolution of my tale, for the chaplain is arrived and sits before me. He tells me my captain is now dead! He swears that he saw him hang twice as, by the grace of God, the rope at first did break; and yet now he swings gibbeted above the swirling river of London for all to see. I must quickly put aside my grief for the sake of posterity, for the children of others, for I will have none of my own, and my time is short.

There were those aboard whose loyalty need be rewarded and when we struck the Caribbean, Kidd did right by those who had stayed at his side. With their share of plunder, and more, these men were dismissed and made their own way to the colony. The ship was cached and a small sloop purchased in its place in which we placed a treasure trove, the great sum of all our travels, in gold and silver, enough to please a king; my captain bid me leave, yet I said that I would stay with him in this to the last.

Thereby, it was Kidd and I, alone, that made landfall upon Gardiner's Island, off East Hampton, nearby New York, and we buried treasure there.

I believe the captain had hopes the location of this trove could be used to bargain our way out of the noose. With what perfidy did the governor, with promises of clemency, lure us - for I refused to leave him - to Boston, where we were arrested; the captain informed him where certain treasure could be found. It was instead secured as evidence against us! It was a hard year in Stone Island for us before we, with others of our mates, were shipped to England and there the Admiralty Court, dire and solemn, pronounced my captain murderer and the whole of us pirates, to be hung by the neck until dead.

I fear not my fate. If my hand now shakes it is not because Execution Dock awaits, but it is in haste that I may finish my story; the chaplain raises his head at the sound of marching feet!

Two things must I say. For those of you dismayed that His Majesty made seizure of our trove I leave you with hope, and dismay. Hope, as the treasure lost was but one tenth part of that we buried; there can be more than one cross on a map and more than one map. Dismay, for when I am gone, I take these places with me and you may dream and you may seek, and this seeking may lay hold of you.

For myself, I think of Father, dear, as I should have done more frequent. And I think of Kidd, my captain who at the last looked me in the eye for long moments, then nodded and spoke my name as my father once did; and he clasped my hand in much the same way.

THE ARTIST

My wife no longer has any great expectations of me, though she loves me dearly. She is good- humoured when she calls me a 'jack of all trades' with the implication, correctly observed, that I am, in fact, a master of none. I draw well, but not superbly; I write short stories that amuse and occasionally move, but never astound the reader; and I play the piano, reciting pieces in such a way that she once drily informed me she was delighted I could play all of the notes comprising Beethoven's *Turkish March* and that if only they had been in the right order, she would have been in raptures.

I can philosophise too, in a bar room sort of way, as you can tell because I am doing it now, and I would be very fit physically, were it not for my weak knees. In short, I am fairly average for my 54 years: average in health and in experiences. My wife has learned to live with disappointment and the unlikelihood that I will have any impact on anyone, other than those closest to me.

We are content though, there's the nub of it: we are homely, yet we enjoy our excursions. If I treat her to a trip out which delights her, she repays me by giving me fish fingers, mash, and beans for tea. That is not a punishment, I promise you; I genuinely love that meal!

If there was one regret that Jean hid well but was discernible to me, it was that she believed I had betrayed my skill as an artist; I say 'skill' because I believe that I have no masterful talent for it. I can sketch well enough, I have a good eye, a reasonable memory, and I am proficient with watercolour although I could never get to grips with oils. I suppose that when we first met on the banks of the Darent under a Kentish sun that glistened upon the water, and she smiled as she watched me work at my easel, she may have thought she had met someone who would make something of himself in the artistic world. The years lingered but have somehow been swept behind us, and life proved her wrong.

But let me tell you of something that in a small way changed her view of me, and my view of myself:

With some frequency, but not often enough, we visited the cultural hub that is London; the breadth and depth of artistic endeavour, be it at the theatre or in the galleries, pulled us from the beautiful and worthy Kent coast which we adored to the hum and bustle of the capital. It was rare that we did not attend a major exhibition at the Tate or the National, but we also took delight in new work from fresh and budding artists. It was this that took us by train to London in May '01, the new millennium spring day crisp and fine with a watery, yellow sun and a light breeze, and to the Forth Street Gallery in Soho.

Now, the gallery is one of those contemporary establishments in the heart of London housing the sort of things that fail to pique my interest: enamelled ceramics, hand-dyed velvet, cows' udders...you get my drift... all very meditative and introspective but give me a landscape or a portrait any time. For once, that is exactly what we were looking forward to as the reviews were heralding a young artist who was either a woman of Kent or a Kentish woman; in any event she currently lived and exhibited on the Folkestone coast, and was just making her mark on the metropolitan scene. This was no sudden bursting forth: as any writer, musician or artist will tell you, overnight success can take 10 or 20 years. The critics, however, had finally cottoned on and viewed her combination of impressionism and figurativism in a favourable light. I, as with many a man, know what I like, and when we entered the gallery, I was struck favourably by what I first saw by the artist Rachel Morris.

My wife, being someone who often prefers to appreciate art alone in her aficionado way, and flits from one exhibit to another, wandered away and left me to my own devices. I like to do things in an orderly fashion and intended to absorb *Beginnings: New perspectives on old faces* as the artist intended, from the beginning—so that is where I began.

There were three rooms exhibiting her work: two small and one large. As it was mid-week, the number of visitors was encouraging but moderate, which was how I preferred it, so I was able to peruse in a leisurely fashion. The paintings, which were overwhelmingly portraits with the occasional landscape, were often vivid yet subtle and I recognised some famous faces, both celebrities and historical; there were those who I knew at first glance, and others only after careful scrutiny. Oddly, as I moved through the rooms, every now and again there was a feeling that

I had seen a face before, but I could not quite place it. This was intriguing yet disconcerting and so I toured with a slight but distinct feeling of déjà vu. I thought that perhaps it was because the talent of Miss Morris was not so original after all. There was the occasional hum of conversation, and once or twice I would exchange comments with a fellow observer as we stood beside each other looking at a work; ahead of me, in the largest room, I caught a glimpse of my wife equally absorbed. All of a sudden, she stopped, and I could see her gazing closely at a painting for a few minutes before she moved on, looking thoughtful and shaking her head. I smiled and, with curiosity, quickened my steps to catch her up; I had noticed over the years that there weren't too many things that puzzled my wife.

With the largest gallery having a skylight that swept upward and was domed overhead, the light from that watery sun, now at its zenith, was magnified and cascaded along the walls. The paintings themselves looked more vibrant and the portraits more like their subjects: every line and stroke were clearly defined and whether they were in reality old or young, handsome or not, those likenesses were strikingly reproduced within the confines of the frame. There was certainly less impressionism than figurativism, but there was still an ethereal quality about them and I could now see why Miss Morris was so highly praised. I stopped to look at the painting that had caused my wife to shake her head; I frowned and peered more closely, then stepped back. The feeling of déjà vu was greater and I turned to look for my wife to call her back.

The sunlight, sweeping forward along both of the walls, then drew my eyes towards a large painting hanging in a prominent position; I wondered whether this was by the design of the artist— I rather felt that it was. In front of the life-size painting, which was of a slim man with a dog, I could see few other details from where I was, stood my wife. As I came up to her, she turned and said in her dry and understated manner,

'Why are there paintings of you in the Forth Street Gallery?'

Well, I think I was justified in allowing my jaw to drop a smidgen or two, and when I felt a hand touching me lightly on the shoulder and found a slender woman of pale beauty with red hair that streamed wildly outwards like a copper corona, my jaw dropped even further because she smiled and spoke quietly with humour, 'Do you recognise yourself?'

My wife looked at me and raised an eyebrow.

'Good God!' I managed.

*

It was the summer of 1976: in the UK, those of a certain age will recollect parched grass, hosepipe bans, and suffocating heat, while those who were children will recall that they woke day after glorious day to a golden sun that inched across a cobalt sky; it seemed that night was put on hold for as long as they swam, played, and laughed.

I met a child, she seemed lonely, (but precocious and entrepreneurial I found) as I descended along a gravel and pebble-studded path from the cliff-top at Leas in Folkestone down to the sea. The path abruptly opened out onto a terrace of small council houses along a road that seemed little used to me, but it had a pavement and the occasional passer-by. There at its side sat a girl with a bright smile and a cascade of red hair; she would have been eight or nine years old while I would have seemed to her, no doubt, ancient at almost 30.

My wife and I had not yet met and her disappointment with me was in the future, so I walked with a companion who was easier to please: a bowl of water, some treats, and a walk were all that my Springer Spaniel Lily required, and she loved me for them too. I was lighter, slimmer, and fitter than now and able to carry my paints, a small easel, and materials in my rucksack. A day on the cliffs, sketching and painting views of the harbour had tired me, but when I saw that the young girl had drawn in coloured chalks on the pavement and upturned a little bonnet next to them, I could not help but smile; I walked over to examine the drawings more closely.

Well, if I was expecting a child's naive scrawlings I was wrong, some of the subject matter may have been that of a child's imaginings: a castle and trees, but there was also a perfectly-proportioned woman's face, young but haggard, and a lifelike cat (the cat itself sat lazily on a nearby wall clearly unaware of its modelling role). The wonderful execution of it all left me rather speechless; I regarded the drawings in amazement and hardly heard when the girl asked me if she could stroke Lily.

40

'Hmmm? Yes, yes...' I answered and then went on, 'Your drawings are lovely. Where did you learn to draw like this?'

She continued to pet Lily and was casual in replying that she had always been able to draw, for as long as she could remember. Then she suddenly looked up and said fiercely,

'I'm going to be an artist when I grow up, when I get some proper paints.' Then she winked and nodded at her bonnet.

Laughing, I said, 'I see. Well, let me help.' I pulled out a pound note and placed it in the bonnet, she looked at me in a slightly disgusted way, so I added another and she winked again.

I took another look at that cat on the wall and the picture on the floor and when I glanced up, hanging over the nearest garden gate was a woman whose likeness to the chalk portrait almost made me draw in my breath. Something told me that this was the young girl's mother and it seemed to me that there was a story behind them, which I knew without being told: the father gone, dead, or absconded, and the two of them, on benefits, against the world. The woman, looking careworn, found time to suddenly smile at the girl and she waved back.

It was the loving wave that did it: I put my rucksack down, opened it, pulled out a small set of watercolour paints, (not my best I admit) leaned over, and said quietly,

'Take these.'

We looked at each other gravely for a minute, each studying the other's face, then she reached out and took them, jumped up, and ran to her mother. They spoke for a few moments, her mother looked over at me and they spoke again; finally, they both nodded and smiled. Satisfied, I waved and walked on towards the sea.

It was a half-hour walk along the front to my rented bungalow, which sat as all artist's homes should, facing the sea. With the sea-breeze gusting in and the sun now redder and lower in the sky, the heat was just bearable. After filling Lily's bowl with fresh water, I mixed myself (in colonial fashion, though I had never been to Asia or any further than France, in fact) a gin pahit with ice and went into my tiny studio at the rear. Pulling out a foot square of medium, cream sketch paper from a drawer, I brushed aside graphite scrapings and dust from my desk and sat and leaned back in the comfiest drawing chair I have ever owned

41

(padded back, leather, on wheels), and for a full two minutes closed my eyes. When I picked up my pencils, I was ready to draw, both upon my memory and upon the paper, an image of that little girl with her untamed hair, dried and crimped in the sun, innocent of face and precocious of heart and talent. When I had finished, I held it up in light now beginning to fade from the window and studied it carefully; finally, I nodded, and with a flourish inscribed it simply *Girl on Street*. Placing it in a buff folder containing an assortment of sketches, I mixed myself another drink. I never saw the girl again.

*

Until now.

What has 24 years brought? A wife, who loves me and who has forgiven any disappointments, two children, a number of dogs (Lily has long gone to that studio in the sky), and, a contented, unassuming happiness. Now, unexpectedly, I have something else to add: satisfaction; for Rachel kissed me (while my wife looked on, no less!) and thanked me for my kindness on that summer day. I looked around the room at my several likenesses which she had returned to over the years when the mood took her, and I laughingly said to Jean,

'Who would have thought I was the muse for a great artist?'

My wife, ever deprecating as far as I am concerned, merely murmured, 'Oh shush, you old fool.'

But she smiled as she spoke and squeezed my arm with warmth; I knew that there would be fish fingers, mash, and beans for tea this evening.

I looked again at the painting of myself and Lily.

The title was merely *Man on Street*.

SINNER MAN

They called him the Preacher. This was only partly on account of his demeanour, which many would say was more akin to a pastor, an ostensible shepherd of men, humble, sober, upright and peaceful in manner. No, they called him Preacher because when he leased them a gun, he would often give a ready quote, if any would listen, sometimes even pulling a tiny New Testament from his pocket. Often the quote would be gentle, at odds with the violence that the gun he hired out or sold was to dispense. Commonly, he would shake his head with regret and murmur, *'Romans 12, Verse 19 – Vengeance is mine saith the Lord.'* At other times, for trusted visitors to his lock-up in one of the back streets of Stockwell, he would extract a large, red Bible with gold lettering from a drawer. It was with a stony eye and an iron voice that he would calmly quote something he deemed relevant from the older, more bombastic books of God; the tempestuous ones. On other occasions he would nod almost in approval as he quoted Exodus 21, *'But if there is harm, then you shall pay life for life, eye for eye, tooth for tooth...'.*

This made even the violent gangs of South London with whom he dealt somewhat wary, there is nothing to rival what some consider madness to create apprehension, but they were prepared to overlook his strangeness as he could provide them with what they wanted, when they wanted it. Some angrily advised him to, *"Shut the 'f' up"*, while others merely grinned, albeit with a nervous, sidelong glance. They recognised, however, that he was as hypocritical as the worst of them, and they were certainly not beguiled by the placid face and the large spectacles which adorned it. When he pushed his glasses to the top of his wiry, black hair, they looked into his eyes and found that they were burnished with common avarice. These violent, acquisitive men recognised one of their own. His soft Jamaican patois, too, could not fool them. He was peculiar, but he was also greedy, calculating and cold.

In only one respect was he none of the above, at least in his own mind. He classed himself as a family man. One could debate

43

whether this was yet another sign of a duplicitous disposition, but those who knew him well, and there were very few, were always genuinely surprised when they viewed the affection he showed to his wife and daughter within the confines of his home. Having exchanged a tool of violence for currency earned no doubt *through* violence, he returned unconcerned to commonplace surroundings in a ragged but clean enough council flat, with no evidence of any remorse that his trade could shatter other lives.

On those rare occasions when he reflected upon these matters, he considered those with whom he dealt as the detritus of humanity. It was his objective to eventually take his family away, leaving the scum behind. He did not ask what the weapons he supplied were used for, he was wiser than that and, to be frank, did not care either. He understood the culture of respect and disrespect, of perceived slight and revenge, of drugs and addiction, of authority and rebellion, and turf wars, and a multitude of other things that caused one person to want to hurt another, but he pushed these thoughts into the back of his mind. He knew that these things were at odds with the teachings he professed to believe in, those that he nodded to enthusiastically at the Pentecostal church on a Sunday, and which as a lay preacher he expounded at the same church. All that concerned him was how much they would pay him, even as he recognised that those coming to him were becoming younger, not much more than children. It seemed sometimes that they were little older than his daughter.

It was of his daughter that he thought, as he always did, as he returned home one evening and rose in a lift, as confining as a coffin, to the 6th floor. It was possible to look out at that height across the estate and take in the street lights as they began to glow with an orange neon, which was never quite enough to push back the shadows. In these shadows, in cold, unlit porches and stairwells, those of a nefarious nature would congregate by twos and threes, never totally comfortable with themselves or with the company they kept but who, with an edgy togetherness, faced the world.

Released from the lift, he stepped onto the landing, which in the semi-gloom took on the quality of a netherworld. Following his usual routine, essential for his peace of mind, he trod softly and looked carefully about him, finally making his way to the large landing windows. The bulk of The Rise, all 16 concrete floors of it, dominated the estate but encircling it, and alongside smaller examples of misguided '70s social housing, ran a small network of roads with inapt names: Eden Street, Paradise Crescent, Halcyon Close. More appropriate was Revelation Road which lay directly beneath him wherein the Preacher, when in sardonic mind, could well envisage the end of days taking place or at the least, beginning. There were no unknown cars parked below or covert figures sliding into the gloom. This was what he feared, whether they be police or foes of a deadlier persuasion, perhaps those who viewed his objective provisioning of weaponry in a vengeful light. It would be of no avail for him to maintain that it was all in the line of business if this had resulted in the loss of a friend, a loved one, or a gang member, occasionally these could be one and the same. In truth, it was not for himself that he feared.

Satisfied, he turned to one of the three doors on the landing. It occurred to him, not for the first time, that his neighbours, two decent Caribbean families of the *Windrush* generation who nodded pleasantly whenever they passed, would no longer be so amiable if they knew who and what he was. When he had slipped his key into the lock and pushed open the door, he stopped for a moment as he always did in the tiny passage and listened. It was often his favourite moment of the day, dependent upon whether his work allowed him to return at hours that were normal, for he would frequently hear his nine-year old daughter laughing as she played, and a smile, which would have looked alien to those on the streets, would broaden his face as he then strode into a living room which was snug, warm and vibrant with colour.

A lady dressed almost as colourfully as the room, with a green and gold woven *Kente* skirt and a white blouse that contrasted with the darkness of her skin, rose sedately and greeted him with a smile almost as broad as his own. The child, dark, with braided hair flying behind her, leapt to her feet and threw her arms around him calling, "Daddy!" The word thrilled him as it always did, and thereafter the evening had an air of normality that belied his world outside; the sharing of food at the table, the talk of

45

homework, a few games, the anticipation of quiet time with his wife when Abigay had been persuaded to go to bed. As he stood over her, ensuring that the blankets were closely folded about her person, her eyes closed and face virtuous, so far from the world within which he lived and dealt, he shivered with a kind of misgiving, unusual for him; when his mobile phone rang. He was tempted to ignore it, but instead frowned and left the bedroom quickly lest it disturb the girl.

This night was no different from others, in that a call could come at any time for a meet, but when he told his wife that he needed to go out, her usually serene face was troubled and she questioned him,

"Why, Daddy?" for such did she call her husband. "Why do you need to go out now? It is cold and dark, and you have us for warmth and comfort. Leave it, whatever it is."

Kristion, the Preacher, hesitated but, putting his hands on her shoulders, he smiled and told her he would be back soon. Putting on a black greatcoat in anticipation of a wind that was now bitter and was driving rain against the panes, he left the house.

He walked in the shadows through the alleys of the estate and was careful not to be seen. The occasional form drew near, indistinct with head down and pushing against the wind and rain, and then was swiftly gone. His own caution was instinctive and as he walked he thought of who he was to meet with an unease that he rarely felt and would never show. Business being business, he tried to push from his mind that Tarone had murdered at least twice to his knowledge. The fact that the victims were members of a rival gang who had no doubt carried out such hits themselves did not ameliorate the crime in the eyes of the law, and the Preacher took it upon himself never to take sides, however in a sudden surge of disgust and scorn he wished inwardly that they would all raze themselves from the Earth as in Proverbs, Chapter 14, Verse 11, *'The house of the wicked will be destroyed...'*

His first call was to his lock-up. Only those few that he trusted came to the lock-up, but Tarone was not one of them and never would be. While such buildings were, for the most part, innocent structures for storage, housing a multitude of items that would not fit in the home, or that owners were reluctant to dispose of, they occasionally hid something darker. His own appeared to be a small garage for bicycles to be repaired, illicitly as he paid no business rates, but this concealed where he also converted deactivated or antique guns to fully working models. He always kept two or three guns ready for use, but he was careful not to keep more than that at any one time. He had a supplier of his own that he used when demand required. Undoing the two padlocks and opening the steel shutters as quietly as he could, he slipped inside.

Kristion knew exactly what he was looking for and where he had hidden it. He left the light off, using the torch on his mobile phone to light his way whilst he removed two uneven bricks from behind the portable TV hanging on the wall and extracted a waterproofed canvas wrap. He opened it up and shone his torch on the weapon. There was a kind of beauty about the gun, whose grey, shimmering steel, while moulded into something so destructive, had an arcane appeal to those not used to such sights. The Preacher had seen too many to consider it as anything other than a source of revenue, but he took a moment to look at it proudly now, a Russian Baikal originally used for firing CS gas that he had modified to fire 9mm bullets. He added a silencer as it would be expected and, placing the whole thing into his inside pocket, secured the lock-up and stepped out into the night once more.

The river was a short walk away, and the moon, when able to force a way from behind clouds that were heavy and dark with rain, rose above the vast supine, concrete dinosaur that was Battersea Power Station, shining a feeble, silver light on the waters of the Thames. Kristion skirted a now-closed park and eventually came to a spot where he leant against the embankment wall, uncaring of its wetness, looking across the river to Chelsea. A man slid to his side and the Preacher turned to him, at once inscrutable.

"Yo, Preacher." Kristion had met Tarone only once before and in the uneven moonlight he looked smaller than he remembered and almost misshapen, hunched as he was in a grey hoody that looked barely enough to keep out the cold. The Preacher nodded.

"You have what I need, bro'?"

The Preacher nodded again. "If you have the means."

Tarone appeared to take offence at this and looking directly at Kristion said quietly: "I always pay my debts. You know what I mean?"

The Preacher murmured: *'So then brothers, we are debtors, and live according to the flesh...'*

The man pulled his hood back and stared. "Give me the goods", he hissed.

Kristion looked more closely at the man. It shook him, though he would never show it, to view a black, bull-like countenance, with eyes that were like knots beneath a high forehead, and a shaven head. For an instance, foreboding almost stayed his hand, then he shrugged and pulled the cloth-wrapped weapon from his inside pocket, holding it out in a firm grip until he felt a wadded envelope placed in his other hand. Each man relinquished their grip and, feeling no further need to converse, Tarone merely curled a lip and strutted swiftly into the murk. The Preacher stared after him, considering that some kind of demon lurked inside everyone, but it was men such as Tarone who chose to let that demon surface, at least when it suited.

As he made his way home, Kristion's unease dissipated with each step even as the rain itself eased, and he wondered why he had felt any misgiving at all. It was merely another meet, another pay-off, further advancement towards the better place that he thought he and his family deserved, and by the time he finally reached home and silently crept into a bed made warm by his wife his misgivings had faded alongside the wind.

It was two days later that Abigay was killed in the crossfire of a drive-by shooting. Kristion, working serenely in the cold, afternoon sun outside his lock-up, heard a bulletin from the television on the wall and then the rushing of feet towards him. He stood, and when he finally understood what was being said, that he was to come *now* to King's College where his wife was waiting at his daughter's bedside, he felt both the heat and iciness of fear pursue each other through his body and mind, even as the car he was bundled into sped through the school run traffic.

Before he arrived at the hospital, the Preacher knew that it was too late for his daughter, for his wife, and for himself. All that he had done, all of the deeds that he had carried out contrariwise to his spiritual and dissembling words, had led to this. He *knew* without knowing that the gun he leased had killed his daughter, and as he flung himself on his knees at the side of her bed, hearing the cries of his wife and the silence of his only child, his mind hummed with the words of Galatians, Chapter 6, Verse 7, *'Do not be deceived. God cannot be mocked. A man reaps what he sows'*. He sobbed knowing that this was but cruel justice for his sins.

SHANGHAI JOE

I knew the original Shanghai Joe. There was another who took that name, but he wasn't a patch on the first, and I heard tell he was killed a few years ago in a brawl down Louisiana way, a relatively young man.

I last saw Joe a couple of years ago, 1878 it was, close by in Charlestown, before he clippered back home to East China and the Songjiang district. He was still a sprite at fifty-nine, cantankerous as ever, and, beneath those hooded lids, his oriental eyes (he was part-Chinese) still threw out that humorous and malicious glint; they told anyone daring to look that here was a man not disposed to dying in a bar fight at any age – no, sir!

So, it came as somewhat of a surprise to hear Joe had 'met Davy Jones' as they say in these parts, and wouldn't be mischievin' anyone anymore.

I was sad to hear this, as me and Joe always got on pretty well, despite his faults – and he had more than a few. So, I was keen to hear the ins and outs of his demise. At first, I could not believe it could be from anything other than a natural cause – no one I ever knew got the better of Joe, at least not for long. Then I thought about them years of trading and wheeling and dealing, and playing fellows off in ports all over, from Shanghai to Portsmouth; and I began to have my doubts. O' course he quieted down a bit when the steamers took over from the schooners – he was an out and out sail man, though he still had to make a living – and only stuck it awhile before settling near the Chinese port wherefrom he took his name; he could never stand to be too far away from the sea.

Anyhow, curious to find someone who could tell me more about Joe's fate, I took a turn towards the Green Dragon tavern, not the same one that was famed for where the *Sons of Liberty* met afore showing King George what he could do with his tea in the harbour – but another in Boston laying claim to that fame. With my game leg (courtesy of a drunk bosun who let off before I had a chance to show him the correct way to discharge a flintlock, curse him!) slowing me down apace, as well as my two score years and ten, it was half of the hour before I had wended my way through the old dock, still loading and unloading and bustling, and came up before the tavern door.

Let me tell you about the port of Boston. The first thing is that it made a lot of Bay State merchants rich; the second is that I ain't one of them. Unless you own your ship, a trade skipper like me kind of facilitates the richness of other folks (curse them!) not his own, though I made a fair enough living. New York or Philadelphia notwithstanding, however, Boston is the port where we seafarers prefer to be. When in the mood for contemplation one can climb Dorchester Heights and view the whole port and downtown, south and west as well, and then there's a kind of mariner community, hard drinking at times, who exchange news, and tell tales both long and truthful.

I knew, then, that when I entered the Dragon there would be at least one or two who would know, or at the least say that they knew, what had happened to Joe. Sure enough, the first person I clapped eyes on was "Red" Ted Ketch.

Now, I ain't a particular fan of Ted, though I can converse with the worst of men as well as the best, most times. So, I looked around for someone else with whom to sit. But he caught my eye and gave me a nod. So, feeling obliged, I asked the barman to bring over a bottle of the better Caribbean rum and two glasses, and I made my way to a corner by a window, where Ted sat smoking a cheroot and taking his pleasure from an ale (although I knew he was partial to a drop of the hard stuff). As it happened, the Dragon, normally humming and busy with mariners, some worthy and others that one might call the human jetsam of the sea, was less so than usual. Ted seemed effusive, at least for him, so I was content to partake of his company – knowing I would hear some news of Joe.

Because it was dim inside, and he sat with his back to the window, the light kind of softened the copper blaze of his hair, though you could still see how he got his moniker. Then I recalled that some said the 'Red' made reference to the blood on his hands; in twenty-five years on the seas, enemies as well as comrades come easy, and the law ain't quite so particular or powerful in the middle of the Pacific; if orders ain't obeyed or things cut up rough, a little spilling of blood is inevitable. No one could say for sure that Ted hadn't stepped over the mark on occasions; most took care not to cross him, as he never forgot a slight. Still, in his way, he was as good a skipper as sailed or steamed, and when not in his cups was fair enough to his men.

The barman himself, not being busy, brought my rum and glasses; I meant to be on Ted's right side if I was to get the lowdown I wanted, so I poured him a generous measure and started right in:

'I heard Joe, as comes from Shanghai, has met his maker?'

'Oh?' Ted says, nonchalant like.

'Now come Ted', says I, 'don't play the innocent. You are still owner and skipper of the *Sussex*, ain't you? I watched her steam in past Castle Island and drop anchor but two days ago. Where else have you come from with a clipper load of tea and silk but the Chinas?'

He shrugged, 'Well, Joe is gone and that's a fact.'

It suddenly came to mind that Ted and Joe hadn't exactly seen eye to eye on more than a few occasions – it was either money or women that got between them – so I guess it wasn't surprising that his regard for that particular seadog's expiry was lacking something on the sympathetic front. I began to think I wasn't going to learn too much in view of his indifference, then something seemed to strike him as amusing and he abruptly opened up with a bit more relish. He was a good-looking fellow, as was Joe, but when he laughed there was something of the sea sprite about him – perhaps it was the devil in him that women found attractive.

Anyhow, from all he said, in between replenishments at my expense, I gathered the following, and I judge it to be the sort of thing that just would happen to Joe, though age must have finally slowed his wits to let it do for him.

The last time I was in the Chinas, I had docked at Shanghai to drop a schooner full of cotton yarn and take on board a load of tea in return. At that time, Joe was shacked up in a tiny s*hikumen*, or terrace, not too far from the Wusong Port. But since then some lucre must have come his way, for Ted said that latterly he had moved to a larger one, out of sight of the sea, but close enough for him to smell the salt and, more importantly, to watch the comings and goings if he had an inclination to take a stroll to the docks. Despite his mixed blood, he lived in the American settlement, one of the foreign enclaves set up after the Opium Wars, and took full part in any licentious goings-on – and there were plenty.

Now, Shanghai not only attracted the decadent, but also the wealthy and those who would become so, and o' course those hangers-on who might also benefit; this included the women, who if respectable might find themselves a husband, and if not, a brothel in which to work. I do many souls an injustice here, because there were those who were honest and worked hard, although they generally stayed poor. Amongst the latter, two sisters and their father disembarked one day from the Hainan Islands, some 800 miles south. This was a long way to come, but their father had some skill as a cook and with a little capital, no doubt scrimped over many a year, took to setting up a restaurant, and with his skill and the attractions of his two girls it began to flourish.

I say 'attractions', because by Ted's account these girls were of the beauteous type and it was moot as to whether it was the food or the girls that pulled in the middling rich; whichever, things were running on an even keel when life took an awkward tack and the father died of dum-dum fever, not greatly common but also not unheard of in those parts.

The girls being left high and dry without their father's acumen and culinary skill, things could have taken a nasty downward turn – but for an admiring benefactor who took a liking to the girls, installed a new cook and generously paid the rent. After a few months, things picked up once more.

Now it is that Joe comes into the tale, for if there is one thing that he likes more than money it is women; when that combines with good food there ain't no stopping him. In the course of one of his evenings, he calls in at this restaurant and takes a fancy to the girls; first off, he plain couldn't resolve which sister to set his seaman's hat at, but at last he settled on Ru Shi.

It was at this point in his telling that Ted set to chuckling, which annoyed me somewhat as I couldn't see what there was to laugh at; and then I saw that there was something of a mean pitch to it, which both puzzled and worried me. It occurred to me that Ted disliked Joe more than I realised. I couldn't think why, until I brought to mind that Joe did the dirty on Ted with a girl down in Newburyport, took her away they say, and if Ted has a heart to break – some say he doesn't – it was broke then. I thought, *dislike ain't a strong enough word for what Ted feels about Joe, no sir!*

Feeling irritated then, but still curious, I chided Ted to get to talking again.

Joe, as I said, was still a handsome fellow. He had a tall bearing and a full head of hair, and those glinting, devilish eyes, and he had taken to looking smart-like, now that he was finally out of those seaman's clothes that the sea and salt had worn to threads. So, it seems he didn't have much trouble in attracting Ru Shi. After eating hours were over, and all the serving and clearing up had been done, she would go to his place; it was common knowledge, but Joe being a man and single and she a girl without any paternal discipline, it seemed an arrangement that suited both and no business of others.

'She was good looking, you say?' I asked Ted.

'Both wondrous', he replied, and he laughed. 'You couldn't choose between 'em. But it was Ru Shi that took his eye of the two.' Then Ted said something that struck me as odd. 'What he didn't know, was that they had a touch of Malay blood in them on their mother's side.'

'Oh?'

Ted showed his teeth, but I wouldn't call it a smile as such:

'That kind of mixed blood has a devilish streak. Treat the women right and you couldn't ask for anyone more loyal. If you are generous with them, they'll do anything for you.'

'Anything?'

'Anything. Treat 'em wrong though, and God help you.'

'What has this to do with Joe?' I was getting impatient now, but Ted suddenly came straight to the point and it shook me.

'Joe had an old char woman who cleaned for him; he was used to having others swab for him, and he weren't going to start himself at his time of life. Anyhow, she knocks one morning and getting no reply opens up... there he lay, face-down on his bed and stock still, naked from his pants up and his back swamped with blood; it had stopped seeping, but the floor was stained vastly with the flood of it. There was no knife, but it didn't need a medic to see what had caused it. A more lifeless *jack-tar* you couldn't imagine.'

'You don't mean…?'

'Joe always was a tad too greedy and never satisfied with his lot. I know that myself…', and Ted sounded as bitter as I've heard him. 'Some say he took up with the other sister as well, and there ain't too many women as are going to put up with that on the sly.'

'So, Joe reckoned the other one better looking in the end after all!'

Here Ted gave out a great guffaw; I could see now that he'd been leading up to this. Reaching inside his greatcoat, he pulled out a photograph, slightly grainy and dark, but plain enough to see the two women dressed in traditional *cheongsam*, but closer fitting around the waist. Their hair looked silken and as dark as two ravens and they had flawless, porcelain Chinese features, although something about the eyes and cheekbones made me think back to what Ted had said about them having Malay blood; they were beautiful indeed, but that weren't why I caught my breath.

'Twins, by God!' I let out.

'Ru Shi and Qing Shan. As alike as two pearls in an oyster,' said Ted, 'Two lovely pearls.'

'Well, which one of them killed Joe? I'm guessing that she has swung for it.'

'There's the rub. There were plenty saw one of them enter Joe's that night – but none could swear to which one.'

'Surely that don't matter, Ted? One of them did it!'

'Well no one knew which – and the Shanghai Mixed Court couldn't figure that one out either; it had to let 'em both go. It ain't the first time it's happened, I read about some such case a while back, in California. If you can't swear by the killer…well, they are scot-free…and I for one am glad of it.' And Ted downed his rum with a satisfied snort.

I stood up to leave. 'Well, Ted, I'm obliged for your tale, though it's a damned odd one at that', and I shook my head. I had reached the door before something struck me and I turned back and asked him how he came to carry their photo on his person.

He stared at me with eyes like a dead fish and said nothing until it came to me:

'*You* gave them the money to keep them afloat!'

His lips curled ever so slightly at the edges and I went on quiet-like, because I didn't care to say exactly what I was thinking:

'You say they would do anything for the man that treats them right?'

He turned his empty glass upside down on the table and said:

'*Anything.*'

I nodded and walked to the door, and feeling his barracuda eyes on my back I was sorely pleased I'd never been on the wrong side of "Red" Ted Ketch – unlike Shanghai Joe.

DEATH CAN WAIT

Old Mr. Death, he's an impatient so and so. You would think not, given that he has Eternity in front of him and a fair bit of it behind too; he has all the time in the universe - he need only wait and he will have us all at some point. Having said that, I've glimpsed him in the shadows a few times when my situation has been dire and he does seem peeved with me – I frustrate him, you see, and he sulks when I avoid one of his snares; I think it affronts his sense of omnipotence.

There was this one, very careless, time that a car struck me pretty full on. It was my fault, I admit; I was rushing home for dinner and took scant notice of the traffic. Meal times have always played a big part in my life, and in this instance cost me a broken leg – it could have been, and probably should have been, worse, of course.

On the subject of food, I've eaten some pretty unsavoury stuff in my time – who makes this supermarket junk? I was once laid up with food poisoning and it was touch and go – I'll swear that I could hear Mr. D outside the bedroom door, shuffling and twitching eagerly. Was that his eye at the keyhole? I'd place money that it was – but I was up and about in a week.

He thought I was toast when that gang waylaid me. I'm convinced he egged them on himself; they would not have realised it but a word or two, unspoken yet still heard, nudging their thoughts, insidiously, maliciously, turning them into violent action, is a distinct possibility. I had walked that alley a hundred times with no problem until that night. Fortunately, I'm as quick on my feet as I am with my wits and I was up and over that wall in a flash – oh, I was long gone, don't you worry!

His obsession with me may have begun when I was very young, of an age when life seems to consist of one long, hot summer; it certainly felt that way – until, out of curiosity, I fell into a cess pit, overgrown and disused. Darkness swallowed me up – and in an instant I knew that I was not alone.

Dependent upon circumstance, fear can hit you swiftly and solidly, leaving you breathless and with a hammering heart, or it can creep up on you gradually - once your initial dazedness slowly subsides and you realise that help is not coming anytime soon. It was pitiful, really, my tiny cries being absorbed into the shadows, but it was worse when I stopped crying – I'm not sure whether I heard it or felt it, but someone – some*thing* - was creeping and crawling towards me. Of course, I know him now, I'm familiar with his *modus operandi,* so to speak – when he is not being quick and brutal old Mr. D likes to feel the fear before he takes you away. He certainly dragged it out; I think he was kind of savouring the moment. It seemed like hours before he was right up close and I could see his eyes glinting and gleaming just a foot from me. My breathing was loud in the enclosed space, but also shallow – right up until the point he was ready to pounce and then I gulped a final mouthful of fetid air, screwed my eyes tightly shut and waited. Then a scrabbling of earth and the blinding whiteness of torchlight signified rescue and I could hear Mr. D grumbling and muttering as he scuttled away.

It's been like that ever since: during the winter floods I almost drowned in the beck at the bottom of the garden; a roof tile landed an inch to the side of me – there seemed no reason that it should fall; a virus laid me perilously low for a month; and …well, you get the picture. Of course, he keeps busy elsewhere too - he doesn't really need me, or those like me, but he does regard us as something of a challenge. But it's getting tough now – I'm not as young as I was.

Today could be his day. The flames are getting *pretty* close, I can tell you. I can see red eyes glowing within them, and I am as aware of his smugness as I am of the heat. I don't know how the fire began; of course, it could have been him, but perhaps I am becoming paranoid. My family are below calling for me to jump. I could take a chance – landing on my feet is my speciality – but the third floor is a long way down even for me, and I can hear the sirens so I know the fire brigade are close. Nine lives is a generous allowance for us cats…but I'm running *very* near the limit now and one mistake …well, Old Mr. D will have me for good. Sod it, I'll wait for the firemen… and you, Death, will have to wait for me.

FOR WANT OF A KISS

When I enter my bar it's kind of rewarding... there's a life about the place that gives me a glow. I tend to weave my way through the crowd looking modest and not too proprietorial, although when I get a nod from a regular Joe here and there – respectful, but not too much – and a smile from a lady as she raises her iced glass, then I do feel as though I'm the smartest guy in the world. In reality, of course, I'm just someone who got lucky. But if I'm feeling self-satisfied, I'll think of Sullivan, and when I do, I am reminded of how often disaster can follow triumph – or, more correctly, triumphalism. So, if there *is* a lesson in what I have to tell you, it is that an unthinking act can bring you right down at any time. Also, of course, never take a woman for granted.

Sullivan and I first became buddies, of the occasional drinking kind, when we ran into each other on Spring Street in '59. It was the kind of day when the rain wet you from your hat down and your shoes up and the dampness met somewhere in the middle; any bar was a port in that storm and when I came alongside one, I ducked inside and shook myself like a dog. With the weekend almost upon us, and this being Lower Manhattan and just inside the Village, I was surprised to find plenty of room to place my hat. The water dripped from the counter to the floor and a lonesome guy on a stool looked up from his beer and said: "Ah, raining is it?"

I took off my coat – it was smart and impractical and sodden – and regarded him with an eyebrow raised. "You think?" I picked up my fedora and hit it against my knee, the spray not quite reaching him.

He suddenly laughed. "Point taken, me lad!" As he spoke, I recognised in his voice an Irish inflection that explained to me why he was quick to laugh and why he had a Guinness before him. He was very handsome, a young fellow too, with his dark hair curled by nature to attract the ladies; if he had one on the scene (and another in the wings) I would not have been surprised. I took all this in on the instant because I'm as sharp at characters as I am in the office at stocks and making money, at least for others. I noted his scruffiness and apparent indolence too, though neither bothered me because I'm of the view that it takes all sorts to make a world; the fact is, of course, that people are not always what they seem, and can be a greater or lesser person than that which you first perceive. So, when he offered me a beer and in lazy fashion called the barman over, I was not as taken by surprise as some might have been when he was addressed as 'Boss' while he was served.

Still, after the beer was poured, I raised both my glass and, this time, two eyebrows, before we drank; he took this, and my glance around the bar, which was itself long and desolate and toneless with a handful of men bent over their drinks, as an enquiry. I was curious how a man of similar age to myself could run a bar in a fashionable city locale and make it so ruinously unpopular; it assaulted my own sense of dynamism, which would never allow this to happen.

I *was* surprised, however, when I discovered that he was not just the manager but the owner, the sad circumstance being that his father, his "Da", as he called him, had bought the bar, using every dollar he had and more, with a view to attracting custom from emigres of the Old Country and died shortly after. For certain his son, Brandon, had not inherited his Da's vigour but instead a love of repose – the world would go by and he would merrily watch it pass, his interest piqued occasionally by a pretty girl's legs.

To be fair, amongst the languid gaiety of this first conversation I discerned hints of earnestness – he was a romantic, which was manifest in his love for poetry and writing; occasionally he would close his eyes and, his voice mellow from the second or third Guinness, let forth with a line or two from Yeats or his favourite, John Montague, a fellow Irish New Yorker who crossed the water to County Tyrone. I did not recognise the words, and yet, even as an ambitious, earthy businessman, I found there was something about them that struck me as being more important than stocks and shares.

Things may have stayed just what they were, a damp Manhattan killing time over a beer and conversation with a loaded Irishman, except that two laughing girls spilled into the bar, shaking umbrellas. Through the open door I could see that the rain still teemed onto glistening sidewalks and the traffic angered itself, the sounds blended together to impress upon us that New York was a humming, moving, city before the doors swung shut.

The silence of the bar didn't seem to shake the girls at all, and one said to the other: "What do you say, Jo, to a Bloody Mary?"

"At this time of the day, Sylvia? But of course!

And they laughed, one golden-haired and the other auburn, and both dressed in that casual but smart chic way of the time, dark striped dresses with gloves. Their clothing indicated they were fairly well-to-do and their manner that they didn't take themselves or life too seriously; of course, if you have money, this is always easier than when you do not.

Looking up, Sullivan suddenly discovered his buoyancy and I think it was a toss-up, at first, as to which of the girls he would choose to flatter the most until the taller, fairer of the two locked her green eyes onto his own of hazel and something sparked between them. I saw it myself and a more unlikely pairing I could not imagine, but in between our cocktails and beers the four of us struck up a conversation that started slowly. The more we drank the more freely it flowed and with dusk arriving early and no work tomorrow, the incentive to leave for an empty bachelor apartment was scant, whilst that to stay was in the shape of two beautiful women. With regards to work I suspected that for the girls a regular familial income was forthcoming, and Sullivan's labour consisted of pretty much what he was doing right now.

The bar filled a little with men, an assortment of the smart and the shabby, refugees from the rain and those reluctant to go home; perhaps a chafing weekend with wives could be held off for an hour or two. The dark-haired girl looked up and about her: "I say, Jo, what a dive this place is! What do you say we head off for something to eat at La Cote Basque?"

From her stool, Josephine examined with a critical eye the bar alongside which they sat; it was unvarnished and the room itself seemed austere to me, a long rectangle full of empty spaces between men at small tables, who were either lost in their drinks or in earnest conversation with each other. The ceiling was low and smoky and yellow. There was an overall lack of jollity except between us four, but this did not seem to bother Josephine and she pulled a lock of damp hair away from her eyes and said, "Oh,

I don't know, Sylvia... see those panels on the wall – solid oak. Floor, parquet. And the mirrors behind the bar. What I could do with a place like this!" She lowered her voice. "Although the clientele could do with shaking up. And the owner." And here she looked directly at Sullivan and smiled.

"Ah, well, you see..." Sullivan halted and then laughed out loud at his own languor. "I'm a poet, not a landlord!" he protested mildly.

"Why not be both? You can consort with fellows of your ilk and make money too if you've a wish." And then she pronounced thoughtfully: "Daddy's a bit of a patron of the arts. God knows he has enough money to give away..."

Sullivan murmured something to himself, at which Sylvia, who, truth be told, found his Gaelic looks and lazy attitude an irritant, told him to stop mumbling and speak up.

He leaned backward on his stool and dreamily proclaimed:

"A little kingdom I possess
where thoughts and feelings dwell,
And very hard I find the task
of governing it well."

He smiled. "Louisa May Alcott, don't you know? I'm not sure what my kingdom is or where... or who its queen might be." Sullivan looked archly at Josephine, who drained her glass and regarded him squarely in the eyes.

"When I find a king, he'll have something of the go-getter about him, I can tell you that." The girls stood to leave when she added, "Mind you, I'm a queen who doesn't mind getting her hands dirty if someone's worth the effort. This is one daddy's girl who is happy to graft."

The girls swept out, taking their lightness with them and leaving just the scent of perfume and a hole in the conversation. I felt it was time to take my leave. Sullivan sat with his chin in one hand and an empty glass in the other. I figured he would be calling for a refill and that I would leave him to it but when at the door I turned to raise a hand he was in that same position; although his eyes were looking at me, they were seeing someone else - perhaps it was a golden-haired queen, beautiful and with wherewithal to boot. I'm not sure.

I stepped out into an evening where the rain had ceased. Darkness had fallen completely, and the city lights glowed like cigarette ends all about me; I too thought of that queen.

*

Business, boring but essential, forbade me from seeing Sullivan for a few weeks but curiosity impelled me to pass his way one evening. In truth, I also felt the need for some light-hearted companionship, the desire to hear a bright laugh and some wit, something, anything, to wash away the weariness of a week in which the importance of profit for clients overrode all considerations – at least according to my boss.

The evening was beginning to darken when I made my way down Spring Street; for some reason I felt delighted as I approached the bar and noticed that a large new sign had replaced the slightly down-at heel and grammatically incorrect *Sullivans*. It was now *Brandon's*, with an apostrophe no less and in the correct place as you might expect, and it suddenly lit up in a neon, shamrock green, if such a colour exists; I immediately felt my spirits lifted and I pushed open the door.

There was a transformation about the place. Things were cleaner, for a start; the ceiling was whiter, and the floor was polished to a light oaken hue. The mirrors behind the bar shone and had the effect of making the whole bigger than it really was. The place seemed more crowded than before and I realised that it really was; it was more than half-full and many tables, each now covered in a green linen cloth the same shade as the sign outside, were taken. More astounding to me was the steady hum of chit-chat and when I looked more closely I could see that it was because the men were no longer of the same morose type I had previously observed; their physiognomy and clothing alone told me that these were of an intellectual or a romantic disposition, some serious in their conversation but not averse to the odd burst of laughter, and with the occasional woman adding to the mix.

Food was being served, albeit of a Bohemian nature: soups of potatoes and cabbage, hunks of bread alongside strong coffee but ales too, and Guinness of course. The lighting was deliberately subdued in places, as if to give intimacy to some of the conversations taking place, but on the whole, it was open and inclusive. The atmosphere was a mish-mash of the cerebral and the artistic and I could only describe the effect to myself as that of a hub; yes, I felt that was the word – the bar was a hub, for whom and what exactly I could not entirely discern, but it felt like a place one could gather for stimulus and discussion with those of like minds. I noticed that money was passing over the bar in just frequent enough a fashion to satisfy any mercenary concerns along with the aesthetic.

When a bright laugh above the clamour drew my attention, I saw with a smile that Josephine had a vivid clip in her short, fair hair and she was wearing a loose white blouse and a colourful skirt in a brave attempt to look sort of Romany chic – it was really not her style. Even so, she sat on a table swinging her legs looking thoroughly at ease and chatting with two seated men with high foreheads and spectacles. Opposite them sat Sylvia, rather less animated, her expression something between sardonic amusement and boredom and accompanied by the occasional roll of the eyes; loyalty compelled her to stick with her friend but she determined to show her disdain for the place and the company by wearing clothes better suited for a nightclub and with the hair and lipstick to match.

I made my way towards them and Josephine leapt from the table with a wave and a smile; Sylvia looked relieved to find someone in a smart suit.

Surprised that either recalled me but pleased to find that they did, when I was close enough to speak and be heard I said: "Well, can I take it that Daddy has decided investment in the catering trade – or is it the arts - is the way to make money?"

"There is no great money in the arts, mister, they just don't seem to go together. It's all about creativity and cups of coffee; if you're Irish, throw in a Guinness. *They* seem to love it, and so does *he*." And Josephine nodded towards the throng.

Sullivan was standing, surrounded, and in conversation, looking happy; I thought he had every reason to be. When he saw me, he nodded and then strolled over, upon which Josephine put her arm around his waist and kissed him firmly on the lips. He seemed to take this with nonchalance and a laugh and said: "Well, me lad, what do you think? We have done well, eh?"

At this, Sylvia inched up to me and whispered in my ear: "I wouldn't take much notice of the *we*, if I were you."

I thought this possibly a little unfair, until I recalled that for someone who had little money and even less get-up and go, Sullivan was now in his element, and encompassed by writers, artists, poets.

"How has this been achieved?" I whispered back.

She took my arm and we nudged our way to the bar, leaving Josephine in her ill-conceived clothes looking up at Sullivan. I didn't think she would ever lose the confident New York manner about her but from the way she gazed at him I could see that the dark curls, the impish eyes, and the full lips, with the romance of verse ever ready upon them, had worked something upon her; she seemed to have forgotten that anyone who wasn't a go-getter could ever be her king.

"Oh, you've noticed, have you?" Sylvia remarked as we ordered our drinks from the same bartender (looking very much more harassed) who had served me before. "Besotted, I would say." And she scowled, "I preferred it when she was the girl about town and her daddy's money was spent on cocktails, clothes and dancing."

"She seems happy enough," I ventured. "Are you not the same for her?"

"If he was right for her, I would be."

We stood with our backs to the bar, she holding a Dirty Martini, and me a beer, and watched Sullivan holding court. I could not find it within me to call him a rogue, for I do not believe he was. He was a charmer – a loveable chancer, perhaps – who had a way with the women and who had come across one, a beautiful one to boot, who was prepared to indulge him. She, in turn, seemed to combine a no-nonsense approach to life with a strange willingness to be seduced; perhaps all her indulged life she had been looking for someone like Sullivan.

The evening flew by in pleasant conversation, not too cerebral for me, and beer. I wondered whether *Brandon's* might be enlivened even further by some music (and thought, if I ran a bar, a little background jazz?), but *Brandon's* patrons did not seem to need it. The whole place was edging towards success, and in such a short space of time too, that I was surprised when Sullivan, as I was taking my farewell of him at the door, voiced the slightest discontent; it enlightened me to the fact, as if I did not already know it coming from a world where money ruled, that no one is ever truly satisfied. This was a different world, with different values and yet he said to me: "Do you know what we need here, me fellow? We need a big name, the brightest of the stars, the best of the literati, one name... people will flock to *Brandon's*. This will be my kingdom, for sure, the kingdom of the painters and the poets... and the potatoes,", and he laughed. "Perhaps even *Da* would have been proud of me... perhaps..." Then he bade me goodbye while Josephine looked across and lifted her head at me, curious. I could only smile and nod; I thought it an odd partnership and wondered how long it would last.

*

I visited *Brandon's* as frequently as I could, mostly at the end of a week when the disillusionment of financial life bore me down and I needed a spiritual boost. This was, naturally, supplemented by the physical, usually more than one beer and, on occasion, even the soup and bread, though I would have preferred a steak. Sylvia, her loyalty for the moment exhausted, was not as often there and I found myself more greatly in conversation with Josephine, which was a good enough reason in itself for calling by - perhaps it was the only reason, I asked myself one evening, as I chatted with her and looked into those blue eyes and listened to her witty talk, not always refined despite her monied background.

Occasionally, Josephine would look across at Sullivan. He appeared to spend most of the evening declaiming to, or in discussions with, an assortment of men and women of letters, the latter sometimes very pretty in the fashion of their type. It was my impression that, though she was still enamoured with him, he paid less attention to her; sometimes she would frown and when she saw that I had noticed this, merely shrugged and smiled so sweetly at me that I forgot my own annoyance at the slight he was giving someone who had enabled so much for him. I should have known that she was not the kind of girl to endure a cavalier attitude for long.

Things came to a head this way:

The evenings were lighter. A walk to *Brandon's* in mild, early spring through Washington Square Park, where the folk singers were in full activist, reasonably melodious, voice, was pleasant, although I arrived at the bar in introspective mood. I knew now that it was Josephine I was going to see, for *Brandon's* I had begun to find pretentious, though still an escape from the culture of the business world I inhabited. And Sullivan himself, although still charming, well… I found myself taking Sylvia's view of him more than once.

Josephine kissed me lightly on the cheek with a nervous, distracted air and whispered: "I have a surprise for him."

"Oh?"

I wondered what daddy's money had provided for this time, and as the bar began to fill and the hands of the ornate, baroque clock on the wall behind the bar moved towards eight our conversation dried up between drinks. As Josephine looked more and more frequently at the door, I began to feel nervous – it was for her that I felt that way; whatever she had planned, it was important to her. It was important because she wanted to please Sullivan, though, God knows, I felt she had done enough for him already.

Sonia Ridger, renowned female poet, entered at five minutes past the hour. Not merely renowned but perhaps the most successful of the confessional school of poets, she was here, in *Brandon's* bar. Born in Dublin, emigrated to the USA, which of the poets present did not know of her or recognise her, though she was now in her sixties, greying lightly? Of course, it meant little to me as I did not know who she was until later, but there was a buzz and Sullivan himself leapt to his feet and watched as Josephine moved to greet her, and then, after a word or two, pointed him out. Miss Ridger joined him and he pulled out a chair for her to be seated, and then he went to the bar, no doubt to demand of the barman that he make haste with the best wine that he had.

Josephine waited. She waited for a wave, she waited for a hug, she waited for a kiss. And when none were forthcoming, and Sullivan was too wrapped up in his own importance to notice, she picked up her coat and tapped me lightly on the shoulder.

"Let's go out to dinner," she said.

*

Let me say it again. When I enter *our* bar it's kind of rewarding… in fact, it's the most rewarding feeling I know, and the woman who raises her iced glass to me with a smile is Josephine, whose name is above the door; we both enjoy the jazz quartet.

I'm not a poet or a man of letters but this thought came to mind when Sullivan, due to his indolence and mismanagement, finally sold to us and went to County Tyrone, in the footsteps of his hero John Montague:

For want of a kiss.
A queen was lost.
For want of a queen,
A kingdom was lost.

It should go without saying that behind every successful man, there is a strong woman and not only that, she deserves to be appreciated; I'm a pretty good kisser, my wife tells me.

UNDER THE RAINBOW

There were five in the saloon of The Black Sheep. Behind the bar, McKinley idly wiped glasses and cocked an ear when the three playing *Irish Switch* made conversation, for he thought he had rarely heard a sillier one; until he recalled that Murphy, Ryan and O'Grady had been at that same table but a week ago. It was always a neat afternoon's entertainment on a quiet Sunday to hear them talk, though Murphy seemed more muted than usual. McKinley was often surprised when a line of common sense was spoken, though it was swiftly swallowed up amongst the babble; now and again he would throw in a line himself if something interested him or he could take no more of the nonsense.

The fifth in the room was a stranger, a little fellow who sat in a corner by the fire in a high-backed chair with his feet a full six inches from the floor and his eyes closed; if he had not moved at times to take a puff from his corn-cob pipe he may well have been asleep. He looked comfortable away from the rain that blew hard against a rattling pane, and the others quickly forgot his presence; they were not the type to have inhibitions at any rate.

O'Grady threw down his cards. "Where did you get that red ace, Murphy?!"

Murphy, sitting tall and straight, less sharp than the others but perhaps not quite as dense as he looked, said solidly: "The same place you got that black one when you were dealing..."

Ryan looked suspiciously at them both and the small, wizened O'Grady quickly picked up his cards. "Foine, foine, carry on, carry on." And he placed down the Queen of Clubs.

Looking at it, Ryan said: "That remoinds me, I saw the widower Byrne in Dundalk yisterdy; he offered to buy me wife."

"Buy your wife what?"

"No, no, buy me wife. Purchase her, loike." He shook his head. "He's mad, o'course. After all, that's bigamy...and I'd pay him to take her." He laughed so much he had to rub his eyes.

"Now, now, that's not fair," said O'Grady. "She's a good-looking woman, your wife, and does do a beautiful roast and poundies."

Ryan looked thoughtful. "So she does..."

"And mine."

"And mine."

They leaned back on their stools as one and thought of the dinners being prepared at home.

"Well," sighed Murphy, "shall we have another for the road? Seamus…" He signalled to McKinley, who put down his cloth and began pulling three pints of the black stuff.

"Speaking of Dundalk, it was the proper craic at the Green Man on Wednesday last," O'Grady reflected. "Fiddler Kelly has a foursome…ah, what a band they are."

"Grand on the fiddle, is he?"

"Fiddle? God no, he plays the accordion. They call him that because he slipped a few punts from the collection when he was warden at St. Patrick's. If Father Donoghue had the getting of him, he'd give him a beating, him being an ex-middleweight from Sligo and all, and ten years in the ring."

"Oi'd like to see him matched against my cousin Slugger," said Ryan.

"What weight is he, this Slugger?" queried Murphy.

"*He?*" Ryan ran skinny fingers through his dark, coarse hair. "*She* is a divil and oi'd geall fifty punts on her to beat any man." He looked nervous as he recalled some distant childhood memories. "There was that time she knocked a tinker down when he tried to steal her peat… he wasn't that sure whether it was her or the donkey gave him a clatter. Mind you, she'd been working all day cutting and drying it and there was no one in this God's green land was going to take it away from her." Then he mused: "What a man, or woman, works for, he'll fight for."

"That's a gem," McKinley thought to himself as he brought over the drinks. He wasn't expecting too many more.

"It's true what you say, Ryan me lad. Look at the three of us. We've worked, haven't we? Let someone try and take what we've earned after the slavin' *we* do!" said O'Grady.

McKinley quickly put the drinks on the table before he dropped them and retired behind the bar.

Ryan reasoned it out. "Well, when you've started out with nuttin'…"

"My exact point!" exclaimed O'Grady. Then he said with pride: "I've now a full-sized bath in the house - but it was in the tin one and outside when I was a boy."

"Wash tub for me," said Ryan.

"Large saucepan," muttered the hulking Murphy.

O'Grady and Ryan stared at him.

"You, you great lug!"

"As a babby I was smaller than a mouse's..." he started.

"Oh, begone with you!" O'Grady said, derisively. "You've made up for it now, me lad. You're big enough to eat the twelve apostles."

"Well... we'd not much in the way of food when I was a cub."

Ryan started up. "We were so poor..." and behind the bar, McKinley sighed. "...so poor we could never afford a sandwich; we used to wipe a slice on a kipper hanging on the door."

"Kipper? You had a kipper?!" said O'Grady, viciously.

"You had a door?" Murphy muttered again. And even McKinley joined in the laughter at that.

With each 'one for the road' the tales grew taller than Jack's beanstalk until at last a blurry O'Grady said: "I've a mouth on me, for dinner."

"And me," said Ryan.

Murphy, who had been sitting quietly for a while, suddenly said softly: "Oi've a confession to be making to you, boys..."

"A confession? You'd be best off making that to Father Donaghue," replied Ryan as he and O'Grady got to their feet, unsteadily, to leave. "For we aren't the sort to keep a secret!"

No... No... it was the talk 'bout the spondoolicks, and I can't keep it to meself anymore... it's just that... oi've come into some money, loike..."

The little man by the fire kept his eyes closed but wriggled his feet. Those standing pulled up and narrowed their eyes; O'Grady's ugly, good-natured face scowled, and McKinley stopped wiping glasses, which already sparkled at any rate.

"You've... you've..."

"Come here to me." Murphy motioned them close and Ryan and O'Grady leaned in. "Gold... and silver..." he paused, "...oi've found a leprechaun's treasure, me boys..."

O'Grady, Ryan and McKinley looked at each other in turn. There was silence but for a crackle or two from the fire, which flared quickly in the hearth. Through an ill-fitting pane, a draught gusted the smoke across the room; it mingled with that from the corn-cob pipe held so very lightly and still in one tiny hand by the fellow in the corner; no one noticed the smoke.

At last, the three roared with laughter. McKinley slapped the bar and thought this was the nonsense that beat all; O'Grady and Ryan slapped their legs and thought this was the finest joke of the afternoon. They admired him for it, loved him for it. Murphy... Murphy, for Jaysus' sake!

Ryan could not stop rubbing his eyes as he laughed, and O'Grady spluttered: "Oh, by God, that was a cracker, Murphy me lad! You gave it to us good and proper; you did. I didn't think you had it in you."

Murphy reddened. "But boys, it's true!"

"Now, now, don't be spoiling a good line, Murphy! I'm off home before the purdies are burnt and the lady lays into me with the pan." And, so saying, Ryan held onto O'Grady's arm and they swung out of the door.

Murphy stared into his glass for a long minute, then swirled the remaining stout before downing it. He looked across at McKinley and opened his mouth to speak but, seeing he was still smiling and shaking his head in appreciation, he merely shrugged and shook his own sadly before standing. "It's goodbye, Seamus," he said.

"You take care, Murphy." McKinley watched him leave and readied himself to lock up; remembering he had a patron by the fire he was about to call over, but the man was gone. All that remained was a small, fading outline in the shamrock-green fabric of the chair.

For one who professed to have come into a fortune Murphy was a sorry figure. He was a superstitious fellow and, if truth be known, an honest man used to his workaday lot in life – it had never consisted of wine, women and song; it was more pints, purdies and the wife. This burden of the leprechaun's hoard was more than he had the stomach for, and he'd heard it was bad luck to boot. Ah! If only there hadn't been a rainbow last week. If only he hadn't the last three pints of the black stuff, which had impelled him to follow in its direction across the meadow; if only he had not used the woods because he was busting for the jacks!

Then he thought of the old saying that one should never look a gift horse in the mouth and his spirits rose; good must surely come of this and he only wished he had taken his find straight home to the wife instead of hiding it away after he had come across it. She had sense, his wife.

He looked carefully about him in the dusk. A donkey-cart full of stones passed and the driver raised his hat in an evening farewell. When he had gone, he scuffed the lane, so normally full of dust but now muddied with the recent rain, and then climbed the nearest stile. As he made his way across the field, still befuddled with drink yet now with purpose, he was oblivious to the soil and grass that clumped on the soles of his labourer's boots - just as he was oblivious to the small figure that followed him. It picked a silent path in his wake, its footsteps in the imprints of Murphy's own.

The copse was a silhouette against the red and lowering sun and when he reached it, Murphy halted for a long moment to take his bearings. The wind-beaten hazel-woods and sycamores combined with elder shrubs closely enough to make a natural barrier but with just enough space through which a man of his bulk could squeeze; certainly, he thought, any of the fey folk would have no problem at all. The treasure had sat at the edge of the large rhododendron to the left, the tip of a gunny sack peeking out inside which there was a trove that had both awed and panicked him. Jaysus, it was as much as he could do once he had looked inside to take it with trembling hands and force his way as deeply into the woods as he could – he had buried it in the damp soil with his bare hands and gone home with a wild head, a guilty conscience and dirty fingernails.

It was almost dark by the time he found the spot and, being the type that he was, a large man afraid of nothing mortal but terrified of the magical, he was unsettled at each crack of a branch or whisper of the wind. He now shook at the thought that some retribution may yet come upon him but he ground his teeth and scrabbled and dug in the dirt until he at last pulled out a brown hessian sack and laid it on the ground beside him. It was heavy, as one might expect, and he thought of what he had previously seen inside.

For the first time something flickered within him, a shadow, and even he recognised it as doubt. As a child, he had always imagined a leprechaun's treasure as being gold and silver coin - not candlesticks and platters and jewellery. He pursued his laboured thoughts further: surely it should be in a pot, not a cheap-looking sack? Then again, for sure he *had* followed the rainbow... but now, hang on there, he hadn't actually reached the *end* of it had he... he was more *under* it... by God, his head was hurting...

"Well, me lad, oi'll thank you for returning that there sack to meself."

The voice spoke from behind Murphy and he leapt as far off the ground as his bulk would allow. Though the speech was made softly, it was not in the way of a gentle manner; it was in the kind of voice that he felt would brook no refusal, nor countenance any discussion about the matter, though it came from a man not above four feet tall! Even so, "I thought they were smaller than that," he thought to himself, as his eyes bulged, and he whispered: Jaysus... a leprechaun..."

The fellow, dressed not much differently to Murphy in the clothes of a countryman with his flat cap and overalls, was silent for a moment. Then he flushed from his neck to his forehead and shouted: "You lummox... I'll... I'm a Republican!"

Murphy struggled with this and shook his head in disbelief. "I didn't know the little folk worried about the politics," he said.

A small foot stamped the ground. "I'm not a leprechaun, you gobdaw! I'm a thief, a burglar, AND a Republican, and if the Guards had not been on me back, I'd not have left the goods where an eejit like yourself could find it."

"You mean..."

"Yes!" the man roared (as far as Murphy could tell). "Now, hand it over for the Cause." And he whipped out a pistol that seemed almost half the size of himself.

Murphy felt a great weight lift from him as he handed over the sack; he even helped the little fellow hoist it onto his shoulder and parted the shrubs for him. "Will you be orlroight with that there?" he asked.

"Sure, I will, I have the cart across the way... or were you thinking I'd be flying?" The man would have slapped his leg as he laughed had he not had both hands occupied.

Murphy watched him struggle across the field then slowly turned for home himself. The thin, red edge of the sun appeared clipped to the horizon, but he knew that in a few minutes he would be left in darkness; only the lights of Dundalk remained to guide him back to a no doubt angry and impatient wife. Yet with a light heart he picked up his steps and hurried home to his dinner.

THE HERON CAFÉ

A solitary rambler, sore of foot and parched of throat, will welcome any haven that promises by its outlook and signage the chance of alleviating those two discomforts I can tell you! I know this from personal experience. Walking alone, seeking inspiration for my literary endeavours in the late summer heat of September 2003, I was certainly sore, and whilst a pint of pale ale would be more to my immediate fancy, at that moment I felt a cup of tea or two, as strong and sweet as you like, would be a welcome substitute. These were my happy thoughts when I reached a small Dartmoor village - pretty much a single main street with a pub and a limited but attractive row of shops and houses - and I saw at its furthest end a small café.

This refuge stood a little distance aloof, a part of the village and yet it seemed not quite, although I could see a brisk enough trade entering and leaving. Upon its shallow, red pitched roof there stood, balanced upon one leg, a bird - large and ungainly with a long bill and which was strangely unmoving in the dull, heated breeze; this made sense to me only when I paused near the door and looking more closely I saw that it was actually a creation of grey steel shimmering in the haze. Its one anatomical adornment was an eye, painted black and yellow which seemed to peer rather sniffily at all who passed beneath and though I have little ornithological knowledge I took this model to be a reasonable representation of a heron; I was assisted to this insight by the fact that the teashop was called The Heron Café.

To be honest, it could have been called The Crow and I would not have cared at that moment; to relieve myself of that rucksack and take the weight from my feet was the desire that occupied me. I stretched out my hand to enter and, as I did so, a bell jangled in that old-fashioned way redolent of teashops the breadth of England and the door was pulled open from the inside; the woman that stood in its frame had an immediate, captivating loveliness. To my eyes she had the kind of beauty that would in all likelihood never be denied whatever she wore, and whether she was made up or not. Neither the worn-out green apron, with the grey heron motif, tied about her waist or the fact that her fair hair was pulled back so very roughly from her face were a detraction - the reverse, in fact, as it made it easier to see her eyes which were of the purest blue. If there were anything that you could call unattractive it was a tired and harassed look about those eyes; there was also an air of anxiety, I would hesitate to call it more.

Is it possible to note so much about someone in so little time? In my sphere of life, it is but natural I am afraid! You could say that such observations – of nature, of people, of the human condition, of beauty, of strength and frailty, let us say of life – come as second nature because an author has to earn a living; mercenary it may be to recycle life as fictional romance and adventure, I agree – but I am not untouched by what I observe if that makes me appear better to you.

If I noticed her it was evident she paid no such attention to me apart from standing aside with the tiniest of absent-minded smiles. Then she walked outside where she looked briefly, almost reflectively in the direction of the village before closing the door and, taking out a small notepad and stunted pencil, she put on a more professional smile and came to take my order. The table at which I sat was in the coolest, darkest corner, which was as well as I was not looking, perhaps not even smelling, my finest after a seven-mile sweat-baked walk from Stickleton. I'll be honest and disclose that even at my best I don't fit the classically handsome mould: in my thirties, with a long nose (long enough, some might say, to take an interest in other peoples' affairs), I was of average height with skin tanned or burnt from numerous travels - travels of which I was becoming a little weary if the truth be told - with my main redeeming feature a full head of dark, wavy hair. Not that she, I'll call her Nicola for that was on her name badge, felt obliged to notice any such things about me – I was but another heated and tired patron with an urge to rest, quench my thirst and sample a sticky bun.

She raised her eyebrows and her pencil at the same time; thereby asking me what I wanted. I couldn't help but notice her hands, small and delicate and white, as she wrote my order:

"Hot tea…" I began…

"The only kind we do," she interrupted, but when I looked at her there was a sparkle of amusement in those delightful eyes;

77

this was far more welcome to me than the uneasy look I had glimpsed earlier, so I smiled and continued,

"...strong and sweet, please, Nicola."

She ignored the familiarity and merely nodded to the sugar bowl and told me to help myself. I discerned the trace of an Irish accent in her speech and when she turned away, I reached into my rucksack and pulled out my own notebook, scribbled and underlined two words.

"I thought I took the orders." Nicola had returned with my tea tray and her neat eyebrows again raised archly with amusement. "And what is it that you have written?"

I looked at the page where I had written *"Gaelic beauty!"* and closed the book.

"Just an observation on the local wildlife." I looked at her steadily. "I'm a writer you see."

"Oh, a writer?" She turned and called out above the heads of the few remaining customers who were enjoying their tea and cakes. "It's a writer we have here Daddy." From the open kitchen a white-haired man, small, craggy, with humour in his eyes looked over his shoulder from where he was cooking an omelette and said in a broader accent than his daughter:

"Is that so? Well, well, we could certainly do with some culture in these parts!" and although a couple of customers looked up sharply at this, when they saw him laugh they could not help but smile themselves.

"In which case I will visit *Old Nog* again," I said.

"Old Nog?"

"The heron from *Tarka the Otter...*"

"I've never read it...but perhaps now I will." And she turned away to serve new customers more deserving of her attention than I.

It was a kind of beginning for me, and as you will see, the start of an ending for her.

*

As September turned to October and thence to November, chill winds whipped more frequently across a moor that often looks forbidding but with its wild beauty never loses its appeal, or the attraction that it holds for me; it fires my imagination with

78

its bleakness. As I walked, I noticed that the nights were drawing in ever more quickly. This did not prevent me from calling in at the Heron twice a week despite a round trip of 14 miles, occasionally by battered car but mostly on foot from the cottage I rented and in which I wrote, often laboriously, in order to meet a publisher's deadline. Each time I entered the village I espied that now often frozen facsimile of Old Nog who seemed to peer at me in welcome from atop the café; each time I saluted him and quickened my step and I recognised that it was not just the exercise that made my heart beat just that little faster.

Frequently I would wrap up warmly, take a seat in the garden at the rear and listen to the small stream, an offshoot of Black Brook, bubble past and watch a real heron, so solitary a creature, stand patiently on its long legs and hunt for fish as they flitted below the surface; Old Nog on the roof looked on disdainfully at this invasion of his domain.

On one occasion, as Nicola brought me my tea, I espied at some distance out on the moor a birdwatcher with his powerful binoculars trained on one such heron feeding in the stream. It startled me when I pointed this out to Nicola with a smile and she gripped my arm and stared intently to where I had indicated. Only when the man turned and headed away did she relax but she did not smile when she went inside, and I was as puzzled as I was shaken.

I saw Nicola only twice outside that little world, that normally comforting capsule filled with tea, beans on toast and a growing affection, at least on my part. The first was at Chigford market where I had wandered in search of something healthier than the white bread and jam which often sustained me whilst working. And there she was, with her father, arguing the merits and cost of out-of-season vegetables with a stall holder. I would say that in the cold, early winter sunlight she looked older than the late twenties that I had her marked down as, but I was never sure whether it was the supressed strain I always seemed to sense in her that was so affecting; despite that, her hair, let down to below her shoulders, glowed sleek and golden in the sun and lent her an air of youthfulness. I sighed and wished that I was not such a romantic.

On the second occasion, we spoke, and I learned more than I had in the past two months of my visitations to the café. It was early morning on my now familiar hike from my cottage to her village, and the frost still lay crisp and silver-white on peat and granite alike alongside the path that I took. Indeed, it was on one of those large, rounded, granite rocks so prevalent upon the moor that I was astounded to find her sitting, one leg crossed over the other and smoking a cigarette. She was wrapped sensibly and warmly in slim-line corduroy jeans and parka jacket with a red and blue tartan scarf about her neck and a grey cable bobble-hat hiding that wonderful hair; her walking boots were sturdy and tiny. She seemed to be waiting for something and I suddenly realised that she had been waiting for me.

Slipping from the rock she joined me and looked up at me as we walked. I found out, during the remaining two miles, that she and her daddy were proudly of the McGarraty clan (motto: *Always Faithful)* from the Irish province of Leinster; that having arrived in Liverpool they then moved swiftly even further from the old country, although she did not say why. She spoke of her daddy and how she worried that age was beginning to make its inevitable inroads into his health although buying and running The Heron was a labour of love for them both.

"You are happy here, then?" I asked.

She hesitated only slightly when she said, "Yes, I am...we are...although..." and then she shook her head. She took out the keys to unlock the café as we arrived at its door and said no more, leaving me with both my writer's and personal curiosity, unsatisfied.

*

It was two weeks before Christmas when I first caught sight of the man.

My attention, as I drank my tea, strong and sweet as usual, was on the fact that I had completed the first draft of my book; it was due at the publishers the next day. This was normally an occasion for relief, if not outright celebration, but I could not raise in my heart the cheer that I should have been feeling. I looked at Nicola as she pottered and chatted almost gaily with a local at the next table and, seeing me observing her, she threw

80

me a smile – for the first time since I had met her, I sensed a loosening of her inner tension. Beyond her, the window steamed up in places on the inside, and so when I viewed an unmoving, dark figure on the green facing the café it was difficult to be sure, in the swiftly fading afternoon light, whether he was watching the cafe or if it was merely my writer's imagination. When I next looked up, he had gone.

It is sometimes of great difficulty knowing when to draw the ending to a tale. The finish is often only the beginning: of hope, of leaving the past behind. I will tell of this particular ending as it happened - and it happened swiftly.

The very next day I chose to visit the café once more; it really was time to say goodbye. Although surprised to see me, Nicola served me with a smile and I sat in my customary shaded corner nursing my tea until the last customer had left and the sun began to fall. When it felt right, I cleared my throat – and at that moment the door opened and a man entered; he was not very tall but was good looking - you might say he was cruelly handsome - with slick, black hair, somewhat dark of countenance, wrapped against the cold in an olive, Barbour wax jacket and a grey scarf. Not seeing me, he shut the door, and turned the sign to indicate to the public that the café was closed; it was the sort of thing I might have written in one of my books.

"Well *Nioiclin*, are you pleased to see me?" This was the name he called Nicola in a broad Irish accent; he looked directly at her and she was as frozen as Old Nog on the roof. Her eyes were wide, and her skin was now like porcelain where the blood had left her face.

Nicola's father came and stood next to her. He looked frail and shook, but had a steel about him where his daughter was concerned.

"It's not here you should be Sean," he said quietly. "You should not be anywhere near."

"Do you think I care for Court Orders, Colm?" he replied.

Her father shook his head sadly, "No, I don't believe you do Sean…but I am phoning the police regardless my lad."

Sean was suddenly angry. "A man has a right to see his wife!" he screamed. At that I rose from my table. Nicola moved at last and put her hands over her face and cried out for Sean to leave her alone, leave her alone, leave her alone…

I have written of many heroes and know myself for certain not to be one - but when Sean grasped her wrists and pulled them harshly away from her face, I saw the fear and loathing in her eyes. I muttered hopefully to myself: *"The pen is mightier than the sword."* and stabbed his thigh with the sharp end of my *2H* pencil.

Sean let go and looked at me in surprise and began to say, "Who is yer man?!" when, I pulled my arm back and struck his face with all the optimism and strength that a romantic writer could muster. It was the first blow I had given in earnest since my schooldays.

I'm ashamed to say that I grinned horribly when Sean reeled against the door holding his nose; he looked at Colm on the telephone to the police and then back to me.

"I will be back, yer man," he hissed.

I walked up to him as calm as you like and looked at him directly in the eye; astoundingly to me I felt no fear and I said:

"No…you won't."

Equally astounding to me, he left.

*

The sun was now red and low, and from the garden Nicola and I watched deep shadows forming the length and breadth of the moor. Within a few minutes, darkness would overtake this place but behind us the lights from the café made it as welcoming to me as ever. I nursed my hand as we spoke.

"I don't believe Sean will bother you anymore," I said. "Not as long as he knows I am here."

She looked at me. "You won't always be here though will you?"

I thought of my manuscript, my love for writing, but also my weariness with travel. I thought then that with imagination one can write about, and from, anything and anywhere in the cosmos. Mostly I thought of the frail Colm and of the beautiful Nioiclin from across the Irish Sea, as she stood beside me.

I watched as a solitary heron dipped its long bill wistfully in the running stream in its search for dinner. A tale of romance would surely end with a second bird arriving; it did not but at least Old Nog on the roof appeared to look down benevolently,

"I've always thought I would be good at running a café," I said with hope.

She stood there in silence for a moment then took my bloodied hand in her tiny, soft unblemished one.

"Let me get you a cup of tea."

"Ah, now you are talking," I said. "Make it…"

"Hot, strong…and very sweet," she smiled. And she stood on her toes and kissed me.

WHEN THE STAGE CAME IN

I know this happened 'cos I was there. Me and the sheriff, and jest about half the town of Oakwood too, an' I guess they never thought they'd see the day when the Jambo Kid was bested. He's back ter plain Jimmy Booker now, though he was the Kid then – the fastest, sharp-shootin' son of a gun I ever did know... 'till the day the stage came in.

This here story ain't got no moral to it, not that I can tell anyways, so I'll just say it how it happened and you can make up your own one if you want. I'm guessing love comes into it somehows, it always does.

First off, the Kid was always a musical feller, leastwise afore he took up his daddy's beat-up Colt and found he could shoot straight and fast, better'n he could sing; but he could play the geetar real nice, and I knowed him as a boy strumming and plucking.

When he seed me, he'd call me over: "Stumpy, get yor mouth harp out and come play!" And I'd shuffle on over, best as my good leg would allow, and we'd bust a few toons between us, his favourite being *The Streets of Laredo*, known otherwise as *The Cowboy's Lament*.

That was afore his daddy passed on with the cholera; it hit him bad and he hardened up then, in the wrong kinda way, and his ma tore her hair out often times, waiting on him to come home, all the while looking out for him while she dug up them old dry fields she called a farm. I'd help out now and again and I'd get somewhat riled at him leaving her slavin' like that in the heat. I'd tell him he was a man now, though he was just on sixteen, and to knuckle right on down, and he would...for a time.

O' course, I knew he was a good boy beneath it – when he weren't shootin' up bottles and practising his draw. In the evenin' I'd sometimes hear that lament on the wind, being played as I ambled back home on ol' Rusty, the slowest and most musical hoss I ever had. He fair pricked up his ears when he heard it, he sure did.

Wiley Bill Dobson and his gang never wanted the Kid for his melodies. They passed by Ma Booker's place one hot day, when the wind was whippin', rising and fallin', and I could see the dust their hosses kicked up hangin' in the air. There were five of 'em 'bout a half mile away and I guess there was a good chance they'd have took no notice of a woman and a beat-up ex-soldier hoeing away but of a sudden the wind dropped like a stone and the quiet hit us like a pan handler's shovel.

Jest for bad luck, Jimmy started his shootin' practice then behind the barn. His ma hated guns and this aft'noon ritual but he'd done his chores and fixed a coupla worn out fences so she let him take down the Colt and holster hangin' on the wall; she jumped like a deer every time she heard a shot ring out and we could smell the powder in the air, wind or no wind.

Them riders pulled up sharp at the sound, their ears were kinda' attuned to the sound of gunplay, I reckon, and they was always ready to fight or run; I could see their heads bobbing round like a bunch of jackrabbits. They seed us and I jest knew they was contemplatin': was it worth their while to come have a look-see at what weren't much more than a large shack and some higgledy outbuildings? So, I prayed a bit, then added a curse or two when they slowly turned our way; but I was quiet when I did so, so's not to scare Ma Booker.

Afore I continue I'll say right now that name don't do that lady justice, 'cos it makes her sound kinda ancient and she ain't that, no sir. She's younger'n me for sure and as pretty as a picture when her hair ain't in them cornflower blue eyes'; it's jest widowhood an' worry and toilin' that puts them frowns on her brow, and when she smiles, which ain't often I'll grant, her face lights up. Strangest thing, I feel younger myself when she does.

I leaned on my hoe and waited quiet, like, and Ma pushed a stray of that fair hair aside so she could see the better as they approached. I weren't frightened none; near four years of being shot at had kinda steeled me up and resolved me to whatever demise comes my way, whenever that might be. I never did unnerstan' that war 'cos when I got up close, I found the fellers doing the shootin' looked jest like me but in grey 'stead of blue.

I recognised Wiley afore he got within a stone's throw; he ain't easy to miss, seeing as he's a head above other folks and as black-eyed and black-bearded in the flesh as on a poster I seed of him once, but far as I knew he weren't wanted in this here state and perhaps he'd like to keep it that way. He was grinnin' with a mouth of yeller teeth and jest the three or four missing at the front; I was hopin' that meant he was in a good mood of sorts, though his son Jake, the Stiller twins and some feller in black I didn't like the look of, all looked as ornery as a pack of coyotes.

Anyroad, they pulled up hard in front of us and I took off my hat to swat away the dust 'cos the wind had picked up again. Still a-grinnin' Wiley looks down at me and says: "What's all the gunplay I heerd, feller?"

"Ain't no gunplay, Mister Dobson," I says, jest as Jimmy lets off another barrage outback; I hears six shots and six bottles a-smashing which gives the biggest lie to what I said and Wiley grins broader still and leans down, confidential like.

"Well now, who's letting off the fireworks back there?"

And afore I could think of anything worthwhile to say, Jimmy meanders round the front with his head down, holstering his gun in a flashy manner. "Say, Ma..." says he, an' looks up. He stops quicker than a polecat in a trap.

I could see a startled look in his eye and his right hand twitch by the side of his holster so, not wanting him to get killed, I says quickly: "Mr. Dobson here was jest a-passing by and thought he'd pay his respects."

"Don't know him," says Jimmy, scowling.

"Not heerd of Wiley Bill!" pipes up Jake. "Why, he's..."

Wiley wags a finger, at which Jake shuts up quick as you like, and, looking amused, he says to Jimmy: "That sounded like some straight shootin', boy."

At that, Jimmy takes the scowl off his face and brightens considerable. "Straight enough, I reckon," he says.

"See you have a Colt 45?"

"My pa's," Jimmy says, and pulls it slowly from his holster; he held it in both hands and as he did, I could see he was thinkin' 'bout his daddy.

Wiley turns to me. "Mister, I'd be obliged if you'd take two of them there rocks you've been diggin' up and place them top of them fenceposts over there." He tips his head at them, 'bout thirty feet away, and when I bends down to pick up a fair size rock he says: "Smaller'n that if you will. Jake, get down off that hoss."

Jake is looking thin and wiry and tetchy as a stoat but grins, showing 'bout the same number of teeth as his pa, and steps down out of the saddle.

When I'd placed the rocks on top of the posts, I stood next to Ma, who knows what is comin' and has her eyes closed. I guessed she was praying that Jimmy would miss, but I looked at that gangly, yeller-haired boy with the steel in his eye and though I didn't know jest how good he was I knew that if pride had anything to do with it, missin' weren't something he was contemplatin'; so I jest sighed and started praying inside alongside his ma.

"Now, Jake here ain't a bad shot," said his daddy, and when Jake starts tellin' him he's better'n that, he directs him to kindly shut his mouth and shoot. So, that lovable character removes his pistol and with arm out front of him takes careful aim and discharges.

Well, it were good and close, but no cigar, as the sayin' goes, and he splinters the wood while the rock stays steady and whole. He gives his pa a sheepish look and Jimmy a good glaring, at which, and with nary a glance, Jimmy fires off two shots close on each other and blasts them rocks into little pieces.

Wiley gives a whistle and there's a general slapping of thighs all round apart from the man in black, who sits quiet; even Jake lets out with a little cussin'. Then Wiley nods to the Stillers, who get off their hosses.

Now, I doubt if there ain't two uglier twins in the whole of Colorado. I was kinda fascinated by their awful bad looks, but I didn't have time to stare too long at their buck-toothed, skinny faces 'cos they picked up two rocks each and, at a signal from Wiley, threw them high in the air. It was like a reflex of some kind 'cos Jimmy couldn't seem to stop hisself; them rocks was in bits afore they was halfway to the ground.

I could see ol' Wiley's eyes glittering by now, and he turns around and looks at the man in black, who dismounts slow and careful, like.

"Well now, son, there ain't no doubtin' you can shoot straight, straighter than anyone I know, but...how fast are you with that there pistol?"

"Fast enough, I reckon," Jimmy says.

I didn't like the way this was shapin' up and Wiley could see I was looking uneasy, so he did his best to reassure me by grinnin' wider still; I could see then he'd got no teeth at the back of his mouth.

"Calm down, old 'un," he declares, which riled me a bit in front of Ma 'cos I don't want her thinkin' I'm in my dotage as well as havin' a game leg, but he carries on: "I jest want to see how he compares to Gravestone here." Now, that shook me a little, 'cos I heerd of this feller and he's got a reputation as a real fast gun, but even more so as the killin' type. "Empty your guns, both of you, we don't want no accidents here. We're jest having a little fun, is all."

Gravestone, who has a face as doleful as his name, don't look too happy about this but I guess Wiley is paying him well so he keeps quiet and takes the shells out of his revolver, which I can see with my army eyes is a Le Mat. Jimmy does the same to that old Colt, which I don't think he'd swap for the shiniest new gun in the West. I know there's only two things he loves more: one is his ma and the other is that cherrywood geetar of his.

"Now, put 'em in your holsters and face off," Wiley instructs. "Further back, get back, ten paces at least. Give yourself some loosenin' room…now, when I hit three you clear leather."

It crossed my mind that three was about as far up as Wiley could count but off he goes anyways, and at three I sees a kind of blurring movement that finds the Colt in Jimmy's hand; it was pointin' directly at Gravestone, whose own gun ain't yet cleared his holster. That gentleman looks kind of shocked and growls: "Again."

Two more times the same thing happened; an', if anythin', young Jimmy gets faster as he finds his rhythm.

Finally, ol' Wiley calls a halt and laughs: "Well, if that don't beat all!" Shakin' his head in a sort of disbelieving way, he suddenly gets all serious and leans right down 'til his face ain't a foot away from Jimmy's own. I have to give the boy credit 'cos he didn't blanche none, though there jest had to be some right pungent breathing going his way. "Would you like to come work for me, boy?"

Jimmy looked as startled as ever I seed him and Ma put her hand to her mouth while I jest held my breath. I heerd the rest of the gang a-mumblin' and a-mutterin'. Then I put in my pennyworth: "Well, Mr. Dobson, I don't think…"

"Let the boy speak, if you please." One thing I will say about Wiley, he's a polite desperado.

Now, as I said afore, Jimmy is a good boy, and I knowed him a long while. I can see what's going around in his head. He's thinking: he loves his ma and he don't want to leave her. On the other hand, Wiley might be paying good dollar for whatever wants doing and he could pass on some of that there cash to his ma. Then again, it ain't likely that Wiley's gonna want him for saintly purposes; yet, digging up rocks and farming scrubland ain't 'zactly the height of success for a hot-blooded youth.

I could see all this churning inside and the whiff of adventure was in his nostrils… jest like it was when I went off to war with a spring in my step, and came back a cripple.

Only when he sees his ma, who has both hands in her mouth now and her eyes wide and unblinkin', does he look down at the floor and says it quiet, like: "I guess I won't take you up on that, Mr. Dobson."

"Say what, boy?"

"Much obliged," says Jimmy, looking up, "but I ain't coming."

"Fair enough." Wiley nods, and regards Jimmy up and down. "At the end of the day you're jest a kid. Mount up, you ornery bunch!" With nary another word he and the rest of the charmers move out in another cloud of dust.

I guess that was the day the Jambo Kid was born. It was a relief to his ma, and me, that he was goin' nowhere, but that was pretty short lived…'cos two days later he ups and leaves afore the sun, or his ma, is up. There's a note for her, in that scraggly, home-schooled writin', saying he loves her and he'll be back. But he was gone, no doubtin', 'cos there's a hoss missin'…along with his Colt and his geetar.

*

It don't take long for reputations to grow out West; most of 'em is subject to what you might call an overplay of the facts, and others are downright lies. But there are some, men mostly but women too, who deserve their reps – gamblers, sharpshooters, outlaws. My advice is to steer clear if any of 'em come too close jest in case any of it's true. It gets so you don't know what to believe no more but one thing Ma and me knew was the Jambo Kid, her Jimmy, weren't no killer; so, when certain tales started mountin' up a few months later, she comes up to me while I'm hauling water at the well and says: "Cole." She ain't ever called me Stumpy, for which she's got my undyin' respect. "Will you find Jimmy…?"

Now, I been seein' a lot more of her since Jimmy went away and I can see her wastin' away. There ain't nothing gonna fully take away that sweet and pretty look she has but underneath she's gettin' sick to the soul with worry. That weren't no surprise: she wants her boy back…but if he's growed too much for that, the least she wants to know is that he's safe and he ain't gone off the rails.

So, I looked at her and said: "I'll do it." Jest like she knew I would, and then she put her hand on my arm for a second and turned away.

She'd had a letter since he'd gone – jest the one – which she picked up from that two-street, one hoss place we called a town over yonder, and I reckon by the time it took to reach there in its round-about way it musta been a coupla three months old. When I read it, I seed that Jimmy is promising to get some money together and when he does, he'll be home; I do believe what was worrying her was how he was going to come by it. Meanwhile, we been hearing 'Jambo' this, and 'Kid' that, from every cowboy and drifter that passed by for the last six months; it ain't a wonder that his ma was sinking.

That letter said he was over Oakwood way, which by my reckoning was about a six day ride, seven on ol' Rusty, bless his hide, and I weren't looking forward to it much, 'cos by now the chill had set in and the same wind that was whipping up dust when Wiley came by was swirling white flakes 'stead. But I packed up all my kit and put on my mufflers and my sheepskin and tied my Stetson low over my ears and set to early next day.

I ain't gonna say much 'bout that journey 'cept it was a dreary and cold 'un, though I been through worse; I was jest pleased to find Rusty on fine form and we came into Oakwood a day earlier than I planned for. It sat in the foothills with scrub oak all 'round, givin' it its name, I guess. The lamps had jest been lit and I could see it was a town somewhat bigger than our own with a saloon and a hotel, a string of small shops and a blacksmith's and a sheriff's office, but it seemed quiet as a graveyard and it weren't long afore I found out why. I was 'bout to check into the cheapest room they had when I overheerd two fellers talkin' in the hotel. Seems Wiley's gang been ruling the roost for a while here, on account they got this gunslinger, the Jambo Kid, to hand if 'n they don't get what they want, when they want it. At this, I picked up my ears and got the lowdown; the sheriff, a goodly feller by the name of Tagg but somewhat long in the tooth, cain't handle it and has sent for a new deputy who's got a reputation of their own... this 'un will be arriving on the stage coach in the morning!

On hearing this I found myself re-saddling Rusty, who deserved better, and heading toward a small ranch outside of Oakwood; the two fellers told me straight off where the Dobson gang was, but, by-the-by, told me I was plain loco too.

I crested a hill round 'bout nine of the evening and when I did, I could see a lit-up ranch house down below; there was smoke blowing from the stack and a smell of cooking vittles', chicken and beans I reckoned, which was cruel attractive to a hungry man, and I woulda spurred right down there 'cept I weren't too sure what welcome I'd get, and anyroad Rusty was plumb worn out.

Well, if it didn't beat all when Rusty hisself picked up his hooves and fair dances down that hill! I noticed then that his ears were twitchin' too and as we got close, I knew why; I could hear that familiar lament carryin' 'cross the vale and the geetar strummin' along with it. Jimmy was on the porch, singing to the moon; his voice ain't the most melodious I ever heerd, if I'm honest, but it's lusty and strong and he do put his heart into it.

When I got close, I heered a voice shout out from within: "Will you stop that damn caterwauling, Kid!"

There was silence then but I didn't get the feelin' it was 'cos the Kid was worryin' too much 'bout what the owner of that whiny voice wanted, who I recognised straight off as Jake. No, it's 'cos he was up on his feet, geetar in one hand and Colt 45 in the other, peerin' out into the dark, and I realised right off that less'n I said something real quick I'm likely to be peppered with shot in an accurate kinda way.

Jimmy got in first with a warning, though: "Get down off that hoss, mister, and state your business or I'm liable to make you sorry for your quietude."

"Well now, Jimmy," I said, "if you cain't recognise me and Rusty here I reckon your eyes have backtracked on you, and you'd miss me anyways!"

At that, he cries out with a delight it was pleasing to see and runs right up to me. I ruffled his hair afore I dismounted and all the time he's stroking Rusty near to wearin' him away; by this I take it to mean he's pleased to see us and when we get near the light, I can see the smile I knowed so well on his face. He looked older and tougher, though not happily so, and when the rest of the gang came out to see what the ruckus was there was a kinda wariness 'bout the whole set up. I got the feeling that Jimmy didn't really want to be there but weren't too sure how to deliver himself from the situation. On the other hand, I figured Wiley was payin' him a good sack of money just to be around and scare good folks with his fancy gunplay. If there was any killin' to be done I reckoned it was Mister Gravestone that did it, and not always in the most straightforward and fair way; dark alleys might have been made for him.

Once they got over their surprise, Wiley, in his politest, most snake-like manner, invited me in to 'splain what the heck I'm doin' there. So, I shook off my coat inside in the warm and took a plate of that chicken and beans and told him about the Kid's ma.

Wiley raises them black eyebrows then and tells me the Kid's doing jest fine and as a matter of fact is goin' into town in the morning to have a quiet word with the new deputy. I played a straight hand as if I knew nothing about it.

"Some are saying it's one of the Earps," the uglier of the Stiller twins pipes up; they ain't identical, you see, they're both ugly but in different ways.

Gravestone looked at Jimmy and I didn't like it to hear him say: "I think the Kid might be earning his money tomorrow…"

"Now, don't you worry," said Wiley, "we'll be backin' you up."

Jimmy said: "I'm goin' down alone...I'll take Stumpy for comp'ny." They all looked suspicious at that but he jest says: "Like you say, p'raps it's 'bout time I earned my keep proper."

Wiley narrowed his eyes, but nods his head and indicates by downing his glass of rye whiskey that we should turn in directly; he kindly throws me an extra blanket so I can fret all night in comfort.

*

This is 'zactly what occurred that next morning and you can believe it or you cain't, but I'll tell it straight and if you want to pass this tale onto your grandkids you can tell them it's true, as sworn by me, personal.

Jimmy and me were up early but we didn't say much, on account of, I figure we'll have plenty of time to talk durin' the ride into Oakwood, and so we sat and ate cold chicken and beans, them two items seeming to be the staple and only things that Jake can throw together for a meal. The rest of the gang joined us, then watched, quiet like, as we saddled up, geetar and all, and headed on out. Wiley shouted out that they'll be joining us later, for which I weren't eternally grateful.

When we was out of range, I was keen to know 'zactly what he's been up to and what his future plans are and why in tarnation he is going into town to have a head to head with one of the Earps, if that's who is comin' in on the stage?

Jimmy summed it up like this: He didn't want to be part of no gang no more and he particular don't want to be near Gravestone. He's got a bundle of cash he saved up for his ma and its in his saddle bag. He's going into town to tell the sheriff he is lighting out and then we're goin' home.

To me, that sounded jest about all I could hope for, though I was wonderin' what Wiley would make of it when this all comes out. Strange, though, despite all that, Jimmy admits to a sneaky liking for him; well, it takes all kinds to make this world is all I can say.

The stage was due in at ten so we arrived 'bout a quarter to the hour and dismounted over by the saloon. There was an uncommon number of bodies standing around considering it was the bitterest morning, but word must have got out 'bout the new deputy and there was a hummin' and buzzin' going on. I saw Sheriff Tagg at the stage-post looking kinda nervous and when he saw the Kid he nearly jumped. He was a kindly-looking feller and I could see why he was out of his depth against the Dobsons. Jimmy was about to go over and put him at his ease when in rolled the stage in a flurry of snow dust and with slush on the wheels and the hosses steaming in spite of the cold.

I think jest about everyone there held their breath when the door opened up.

Out stepped a tall hombre with a black, waxed moustache that hung down either side of a mean-looking mouth and a jaw like a lantern. Sheriff Tagg hurried over and the Kid strolled behind him. Then I seed something out of the ordinary: this feller weren't packing any guns and seemed kinda surprised at the attention. I'm thinkin' something ain't quite right when Tagg says: "Welcome to Oakwood! Mr. Earp?"

The big dude squeaks, "Certainly not!" turns up his collar, picks up his case and heads off to the hotel.

Well, if that didn't make a few mouths fall open; mine and the Kid's and the sheriff's and all!

Tagg called up to the driver, who was about to dismount: "Dang it, did you have Mr. Earp with you?"

The driver cain't stop hisself from laughin'. "MISS Earp is right there, Sheriff!"

We all shooted our heads around and the prettiest young lady stepped out of the carriage, carrying a plain valise and wrapped up to the neck in a brown twill duster coat. Tagg looked kinda flustered with the shock of it all but, remembering his manners, he took off his hat.

"Sheriff Tagg? Winona Earp at your service." She laughed at the dumbfound look she seed on some faces and the downright dismay of the townsfolk; 'cos they're looking at the Kid and the lady and making unfavourable comparisons, and adjudging the prospects for their own safety and future well- bein'.

Now, I think I may have been the only one but I noticed something a bit gritty 'bout that laugh and there were something, too, 'bout the look on her face, which, though of the attractive kind, had a hint or two of steel about it; also, the look in her eyes was right mischievous. I then noticed how the Kid had a kinda soppy look about his demeanour. He held out his hand and said: "Miss Earp, I'm glad to make your acquaintance, ma'am." And he puffed out his chest, which was still on the skinny side. "Jimmy…they call me the Kid."

She raised an eyebrow. "I'm pleased to meet you, Mister Kid," which ruffled him a bit, but afore he could put her straight the sheriff comes right out with what we was all thinkin'.

"Err…ma'am" and he rolled his hat in his hands, "if you'll forgive me…you ain't 'zactly what we was all expecting…you see, Earp…"

"Distant cousins, Sheriff" she said, sharp and crisp. "But you have nothin' to be afraid of with me. I'm the first female peace officer in the West…but I won't be the last."

At this point Jimmy made his big mistake, feeling it incumbent upon his growing-up, manly soul to tell her plying that particular trade in places like Oakwood calls for tough talking and tough shooting and ain't 'zactly women's work. "It just ain't safe, you see." He was thinkin' of the Dobsons, and he meant it well and chivalrous, but she turned to him real slow with a smile and a glintin' eye.

"Oh, I see." And she looked him up and down. "You're *that* Kid, are you?" Jimmy puffed up his chest again then, but I could see he was startin' to feel a mite uncomfortable. "Sharpshooter, aren't you?" She carried on, relentless. "Fast too, I hear."

"Well, I…" began Jimmy, but Miss Earp has got herself into the swing of things right then and she calls to the driver to pass her big case down.

While me and the sheriff manhandle it to the floor, she says to Jimmy: "I'm from Ohio, does that mean anything to you? *Mister* Kid?"

"No, I don't reckon it does, ma'am," replies Jimmy, who by now is getting irritable.

"Well, perhaps I can explain." She opened up her case and pulled out a Winchester '73 rifle, plain with good wood and an open sight. When she pulled her coat aside, danged if she ain't wearing a pearl handled Smith and Wesson revolver. "Got anywhere to shoot, Sheriff?" she asks Tagg, who is going all goggle-eyed.

"Now, Miss Earp, this ain't rightly..." he starts off, but she's already heading towards the end of the street with a crowd following like that piper feller in the fairy tale. She shouts out to bring her valise and some bottles too and there's a scramble to oblige with some empties, while Jimmy dragged hisself along behind looking kinda reluctant. He's still feeling gallant, see, and don't want to show up this pretty young thing; I can tell he's taken a shine to her, for sure.

This whole circus stopped at an old patch of ground fenced in, for whatever purpose, and she entered and called for Jimmy to follow; me and the sheriff, who's looking like the lostest soul I ever seed, took up a stance a few yards behind them, bottles nearby. The crowd leaned over the fence.

Miss Earp turns and says to Jimmy: "Now, pistol drawing isn't my forte, Mister Kid, so you'll allow me to have mine to hand. You can do the same, of course."

Jimmy shrugs and smiles at that and returns that he'd just as soon as draw when ready; he's thinkin' he could put all this to bed with a demonstration of speed and precision using just the one shot.

"Toss that bottle, Sheriff," she says.

That green bottle is in a thousand pieces afore it is half-way up and the Kid's gun ain't even out of his holster.

"Two bottles, Sheriff!" she cries out loud, her eyes a-glowing.

This time the Kid's gun is in his hand but both bottles are splintered afore he can get a shot off.

The Kid is looking at her and he suddenly bucks up, 'cos his pride ain't going to let him be outsmarted or outshot by no female. "Well now," he says, "you've kinda had the advantage, so this time I'll be doing the same as you," and he has his gun in his hand ready. "Three bottles!"

Jimmy shoots one bottle and she shoots two. But she looks admiring at him. "Not bad at all. Though I'm more at home with this." She holstered her pistol and picked up her Winchester, which is looking kinda beautiful 'cos of its plainness. "How's a dollar for you?" she asks the Kid.

"Toss 'er up," he says, and I gets a silver coin out and throws it high, the lady standing aside.

Well, it's a good shot with a pistol and I hear it clink and see it move in the air and when I pick it up it has a little nick in the side. There's more 'un a little ripple of appreciation from that throng hanging over the fence.

The lady looks grim to me but tells me to throw up two and that the sheriff will reimburse me my expenses. So, up I sends 'em.

There's two loud cracks and a whizzin' in the air and when them dollars fall to the ground, I find a hole plumb centre in each. The crowd is startin' to go wild and the Kid is looking kinda despondent but she ain't finished yet. I don't think any of us will forget what we seed next.

Miss Earp, this pretty, tiny lady with the pluck of a frontiersman and the eye of an eagle, looked down along the main street. "Clear the way," she said, and they all shuffled back like a gaggle of geese.

Out of her valise, she took a vanity mirror which, as I recall, had an ivory handle and a not very big glass, but it was enough. The saloon was 'bout a hunnerd paces away and there was a bell hangin' over the door and after she studied it for a moment, she turned her back and put the rifle over her shoulder. Now, think 'bout this, do. She's a-looking in a mirror held in the one hand and her finger is on the trigger of the rifle with the other...and she lets fly.

It took but an instant for that bell to ring. We cain't believe what we seed, and we was quiet as church mice for the longest second that ever existed, while the sound of that bell rang through our ears and took root in our heads for the rest of our lives, 'cos we ain't ever goin' to forget it. Then, we went crazy, the Kid included.

Ohio, she said. Then I recalled that Annie Oakley, 'Little Miss Sure Shot', greatest markswoman in the West came from there and, it turns out, as Miss Earp 'splained, that Annie has taught dozens of women to be as good as, better'n, the men; she's just one of 'em.

To end my tale, I'll just say this, 'cos I don't like loose ends and p'raps you don't either.

The Dobsons had come sneakin' in after the Kid and seen it all. When the Kid and Miss Earp turned to meet 'em they looked beat, even Gravestone, and slunk away; and Oakwood had two new deputies, courtesy of Sheriff Tagg.

On the way back to the saloon Miss Earp seed Jimmy's guitar on his hoss and she says to him that she'd like him to sing to her; at which he asked whether she likes *The Streets of Laredo*. I seed her smile when she said it was her favourite.

And Jimmy gave me the cash for me and Rusty to take back home to his ma…'ceptin' she don't ever let me call her that now; she's my Mary.

HIDE AWAY, MOON

You never appreciate something until you lose it, do you? I thought I knew what I had when I married my wife - and she thought she knew what she was losing when she left me. So, you could say we both thought we were doing the right thing at different times and we were both winners; not so, and I'll tell you why.

We were both from south of the Thames and met in the black and white '50s on a park bench. Battersea, it was, and I have to say that park did its best to splash us all with some post-war colour, what with the pleasure gardens and the funfair and the Guinness clock, which performed its antics on the quarter hour. I was watching it with my mouth open and a cheese sandwich paused en route when Barbara (of course, I called her Babs long before matrimony) sat herself down and after a moment enquired if that same sandwich was ever to reach my mouth or if it was going to stay stuck like that. I looked at her and liked what I saw, so I said: "Well, princess, this here sandwich is ready to be masticated at any time, but I'm happy to share it with you if you are hungry."

And I could see she didn't know what 'masticated' meant and that's what I intended because people take me at face value and can't see that a painter and decorator like me can be educated too – well, when I say educated, I mean that I've always got my head stuck in a book, and I've got a rare vocabulary for a young man of my trade.

When she wrinkled her nose at me, I liked her even more for it and in some funny way it didn't detract from her made up beauty; for that one moment it enhanced it, and I could see beneath the powder and eye lashes and permed hair to what I called a Lambeth rose. In that sense she had a delicate prettiness but a personality with enough thorns to prick your ego. Her smell was smoky and sassy, like her personality, and I thought she was down to earth but I found out later she would never be content with being that. She wanted to rise up: perhaps in a horticultural sense she was more like a sunflower, face up and reaching towards the light; and if she had known I was a pot plant perhaps she wouldn't have married me.

As it happened, we hit it off pretty well; and when you sit and eat crumbling sandwiches together on dried grass in summer and drink tea in park cafes and take walks alongside a muddy Thames that still, in the evening, dances with amber mirrored light, it's not a long stretch to a registry wedding and the sharing of a rented Clapham flat. There the romance is harder to maintain, of course.

For a start, her parents made it hard for me. I could see straight away why: they wanted better for her, naturally, but I think they also wanted to trade up on her beauty. The thing is they were no better or worse than me, less educated in fact; I didn't dislike them but their sort of attitude was bound to rub off on her over time and in our second winter I found her watching me of an evening as we sat opposite the kitchen stove keeping warm. Her face looked kind of distastefully upon me whenever I looked up from my book and I knew she was thinking: "Is this it?"

Me, I felt a kind of contentment up to that time because we had a bit of a garden, being on the ground floor, where we could sit in the sun in the summer; and in the winter I recall we often went 'up west' and looked in at the London stores with their Christmas displays and at the lights, wired but seemingly floating above us, as we criss-crossed Oxford and Regent Streets. On what I earned we were lookers, not buyers - but she was happy until she lost the baby.

That was the start of it - but not the whole, because she had always had the slightest air of discontent; there were times at night when she sat on my knee and kissed me with soft lips stripped of redness or lay with her head on my shoulders, yet others where her fingers drummed on Formica tops. I could see she was vexed because I did not display the same sorrow (though, in fact, I ached with it) but more than that, she reviled my lack of ambition. Each week I gave her my money and she gave me ten shillings for my leisure – the rest she put in a jar on the mantle; I never really knew what she was saving for.

In the third year we began the arguments. This makes it sound as if they were consensual and some arguments are – but mostly they are not. They are born out of one person's anger, frustration, and, sometimes, contempt. I kept my head down when the sniping started, usually after a hard day's work and supper, when all I wanted to do was read and relax; her infuriation was real. At each instance, when I could ignore it no longer, I would put my book down and say to myself: "Oh, the moon's out," an expression of my old dad's, which is to say: *Here we go again...* as if the moon itself were the cause of every quarrel that ever took place.

It got so that I could not help but say it out loud whenever she started on me and she would screech in infuriation: "What do you mean?! I don't know what you mean!"

Occasionally, I would get up and, standing by the window, pull the curtains aside and look up at the sky while she shouted at me.

"I see the moon is out again, is it?" I'd say, and I was surprised at how often it really was.

I came home one evening when it was dark and the cold was biting to find the mantle jar empty and a note underneath it. It wasn't a bad note: she was off with someone else, she explained, someone with a bit of oomph, but she signed it with a kiss and she had lit the kitchen stove for me so there was no hatred in what she had written or done. I tried to detect whether there was sadness in there too, but, bright as I am, I could only read the starkness of what she was saying and not between the lines. I decided I had enough sadness for both of us anyway.

Life continued, of course. The following summer I watched as she floated past me in the park; she was arm in arm with a man who was handsome but spiv-like and who I later discovered was her manager at a department store where she sold perfume. I could not say that she looked any happier but she was dressed smartly and smelt expensive; I preferred the earthy scent of my Lambeth rose. Her mum and dad were in tow, looking slyly smug, but when Babs saw me eating my sandwich she just looked as though she would cry.

Then there came a time when I suddenly became enterprising and bought a bigger white van and hired a mate to keep up with the trade; I think Babs would have been shocked rather than delighted, perhaps, she was so used to my indolence. I will swear that she did not know of this when she knocked at my door later that year; she stood there looking single and rejected, less elegant than before and chilly.

I looked at her, then up at the cold, clear sky. There were stars, billions of them…and no moon. So, I nodded and stood aside, and as she passed me the scent from my Lambeth rose once again filled my head.

ANNIVERSARY

When he saw the woman with the heart-shaped face he wondercd, rather idly, whether it was time for another affair.

Drinking tea, alone, the day after he arrived the Edwardian gentleman had found, to his surprise, that he took pleasure in the experience and so made a point of strolling to the quayside café each day. When he sat outside, the Cornish sea breeze and the warmth of the sun wore away at his lassitude such that he forgot all about London and its excesses. On the third day he saw her.

There was no particular reason that she caught his eye apart from the fact she was a woman. She was neither especially pretty – she would possibly have been called homely were she a resident in the capital, where beauty is measured in a myriad ways that have nothing to do with such a thing – nor particularly stylish in the way she dressed, nor elegant in the way that she walked towards the off-white, salt-scarred wooden rails; it was the way, perhaps, that she leaned forward against those rails and faced the hills and crags across the water.

Seeing that she was not as handsome as the many other women he had known he might have lost interest, but there was, to his mind, something of absorption in her manner as she contemplated the jutting point of land where the calmer waters of the estuary became the sea; and when she turned her head towards him it was her eyes, so dark and almost vacant, were it not for the wistfulness within, that commanded his attention. Those eyes swept through him and over him and past him and returned once again to regard that vista of green trees sloping eastward to where the promontory stood sharp and black against the sky; the sun was nearly at the mid-morning position and shone clearly and with a lingering, early-summer heat.

He could see nothing to attract her attention. There was the small, red foot ferry which in a few minutes made a journey that saved day trippers two hours overland and there was the sight of white sails against the blue of the sea as tiny yachts scudded to and fro – but he felt that she saw beyond these, towards something that could not be seen.

The waitress arrived to clear his table, and she smiled while he nodded, supercilious and polite in reply; it was what people of privilege did and he was rich in money and manners, if not morals. He did not like to think of it often but when he did, he realised that he may be somewhat bankrupt in that area; he attributed it to the fact that although women loved him, he had never loved one in return, and he was not sure if he was proud of that or rather sad. Thus, Mr. Raymond Clifton frowned, and if a frown can be of melancholy nature this one was and so he answered his own question without knowing.

When a man approached the rails and stood next to the woman, Clifton realised his eyes had never left her. It may have been that she had loosed her hair and it hung long down her back in a way that he had never seen in London society, only in moments of intimacy. It was a self-indulgent life that he had led, because it was easy for him to do so, being arrogantly good-looking and wealthy. Had the glamour of high society life flaked off? He felt that it had, at least for the time being; he thought that he would not miss its shallowness for a few weeks and he breathed deeply of the salt air, but still he watched the woman with the faraway eyes and the man who was now close up beside her.

The man, though provincially dressed, was smart in his way, with brightly coloured striped blazer and flannel trousers, whilst the woman wore a white blouse, and no jacket - something which the society ladies would not have dreamed of - against which her hair seemed as black as a raven, and a gently fluted navy skirt which was nipped in at the waist and around which an arm was now proprietorially placed; Clifton was amused when the woman shook it off. He put the man in his late twenties though the face seemed younger when it became petulant and Clifton leaned back in his chair and regarded the pair in a casual manner. The woman was younger but knew her mind, it seemed, because, all of a sudden, the man's temper appeared to break at what she said to him and he took hold of her arm, a little roughly, it seemed to Raymond. He was aware that it was none of his business but he found himself rising and brushing non-existent dust from the jacket shoulders of his voguish, single-breasted light-grey sack suit and staring at the young man.

It could have been merely that his movement was caught in the corners of their eyes but the couple turned towards Clifton and, seeing that he had the authoritarian manner of someone older than himself – perhaps too, he sensed the urbanity in him - the man took his hand from her arm, shook his head, it seemed finally more in sorrow than in anger, and quickly walked back along the quay in the direction of the little town of Lowie. The woman watched him only briefly before she looked at Clifton; this time she allowed her eyes to regard him at some length – he did not feel uncomfortable at this exactly, but he felt that she was searching him from the inside out. Then she smiled and walked steadily to stand before him.

"Thank you...he wasn't right for me, you know."

"Oh?"

"One can tell...you have a kind face, for example."

Clifton was not used to conversations beginning in this fashion, but in any event he really could not see this. He recalled, honestly, his rather indolent eyes and his swept-back hair and the patrician nose down which he frequently looked, but her words were refreshing and warmed him; instead of his usual tight little smile he gave one of genuine openness. For one moment he thought to himself that perhaps he wasn't the jaded, dissolute man about town - perhaps he was not such a bad fellow after all – and indeed it was true that although he had not loved he had not hurt either.

"I..."

You and I, we will meet again," she said. "If you would like me to join you for tea...what may I call you?"

"My name is Mr. Clif..."

She gave a delicate wave of the hand. "I mean, what shall I *call* you?"

"Well, you may call me Raymond."

"Raymond and Cissie...very well, Raymond," and she smiled again and walked away.

This was not how his conversations tended to end either.

When he lay in bed that evening, occupant of a large bed in a small room – although the hotel was pleasant enough and close to the edge of the little town - he could recall her well-spoken words, but rich with the accent of the West Country, and her dark hair and darker eyes. He tried to shake this away and thought to himself that, until recently at least, if he loved anything at all what he really loved was not truly life but its trappings, all that his inherited station and wealth brought him. But as sleep overtook him, he saw a heart-shaped face when he closed his eyes.

*

Even the days of a thoroughly jaundiced man may become brighter, every step he takes less lacklustre, given the right circumstance. Clifton woke each morning to a sun in a sapphire sky and gulls squawking and cawing out of sight and in the new knowledge of seeing Cissie; these were enough to begin a day with a lighter heart. And seeing her was now a regular feature of these days, Clifton striding with more purpose, one might say almost anxiously, to the café, to the beach, where she would insist they swam every day, and to the clifftop where there were walks on the greensward, the conversation turning this way and that in the wind and where, all of a sudden, Cissie would stop and, in silence, for long moments look out across the bay. The summer that had stretched out before him began to compact such that he felt each day was of breathless urgency, to be made the best of and the most of – and he knew not exactly why he felt this way because he had not felt love before.

Her conversation was local and different, often animated, apart from those dreamy episodes, though at the end of each day he did not feel he knew her a great deal better; in truth, and in part, mystery is a promoter of love, especially to those who are used to others opening themselves up with little inhibition. Too, when he was with her, he found she compared wonderfully against those London socialites who lounged by day in their apartments and alternately smoked or lay as inert as rugs before rousing themselves for lunch or evening dinner, dressing in pearls and perfume.

One morning the young man he had seen with Cissie approached as Clifton sat waiting at the café. It was a measure of how much his natural aloofness had dissipated that he was ready to engage in friendly conversation if the man wished. It did not arise, although Clifton was now used to conversations that did not begin or end as he expected.

"She's some good maid, isn't she?"

"I'm sorry?" replied Clifton.

"I said she's a good maid, a good girl, isn't she?" He hesitated for a moment. "Has she told you what happened?"

Clifton thought back to the incident when he first saw Cissie: "Well, it's not my business, I presume you..." began Clifton.

"No, no. It's...I've tried to help her, we've all tried to help her. Since that August month..."

"I really have no idea..."

"She's coming," he nodded and, buttoning up that same coloured blazer as he went, scurried away.

It was an unusual, if not fantastical, exchange. When Cissie drew near she looked after the departing figure but said nothing whilst Clifton poured her tea; he was quite undecided as to his next words. He was suddenly not at all sure that he wasn't out of his element in these parts, though he had always prided himself on being cosmopolitan; for the first time he noticed that the waitress, as she bustled, threw the occasional, quizzical glance in their direction. An elderly couple at one of the other tables, locals to be certain, conversed quietly and did the same. He realised how small a place this really was despite the day trippers and the tourists and of a sudden Clifton felt light-headed and angry – was it the fact that he was somewhat older than Cissie? Was it any business of others? He turned to Cissie with questions and with doubts about himself and about the two of them but as soon as he looked at her, he knew that he wanted this woman, and said nothing.

"What day is it, Raymond?" she said, distantly.

"Oh, why it's Tuesday."

"The date, Raymond. It is August, is it not?"

"Of course."

"The end?"

"Near enough the end of the month, yes." He smiled at her. "Have you plans?"

Looking quickly at him, she nodded. "Yes - for us both, of course" and when she smiled, he was suddenly relieved and put his earlier conversation to the back of his mind. She took his hand in hers. "I know a cave, Raymond," she said in a quiet voice.

"I beg your pardon?"

"Tomorrow will be a beautiful day," she placed her other hand on his, "and I know a beach and there is a cave... where we can be alone..." She said no more; there was no need to because his body and heart were gripped and his urbanity broken.

*

They met at the ferry-side. At midday it was hotter than it had been all of the summer, albeit with a growing breeze, and the three other passengers - ladies, day trippers from appearance - hid under their parasols and chatted; the two would-be lovers kept themselves apart.

The petite and pretty ferry itself was a quiet affair, with an electric motor, and the ferryman was even quieter. He sat in his little cabin and stared ahead, seeing only what he needed to see and with the expression of one who had piloted this short journey forwards and backwards, to and fro, for too much of his middle-aged life. His eyes were rather dull, apart from when he glanced at Cissie and Clifton, who sat in the prow of the boat rocking gently in concord with the movement of the waves. When he noticed the ferryman's look Clifton recalled those of others and the young man's words yesterday - he did not understand what they meant but for the very slightest moment he shivered as if the sun had been taken behind a cloud...

The 'Hill Walk', as it was known locally, was not one likely to appeal to ladies with parasols. So it proved, for as soon as the ferry docked it was a scuttle for them to the tea shop with a delightful view across the water to Lowie. On a day when one perspired whilst merely strolling it seemed the sensible thing to do – but Cissie passed a large picnic basket to Clifton, took his hand and set off with a will along a well signed path.

Clifton saw her stride was confident, almost impatient, and the path was an easy one and very much cooler within the shade of the trees – until she turned aside at a small fork. She still chattered in a lively fashion but the path became narrower and though they were both wearing practical, less constricted clothing and stout shoes, the going was harder with ferns and brambles and Cissie led the way; she wore her hair up and he followed that beautiful, exposed neck in a kind of heated reverie – he thought that he would do so no matter where it led.

When they finally came out of the trees, he felt that the steepness of the climb and the effort taken was worth it, for it was to a cliff top with a clear view right out to sea. His eyes could barely take in the blueness and vastness of the waters as they stretched away towards a different continent, but he was given little time to contemplate this as Cissie stood close to him and pointed downwards, to a tiny cove; from where they stood the sand was a pristine, buttercup yellow and the sea broke between the sheltering rocks right up to its edge.

It was only when they began the steep decline that Clifton was able to catch site of the cave. The low entrance arched the width of the beach and it struck him that, depending upon one's frame of mind, its mouth could either be very welcoming – on a day like this its coolness and the anticipation of what might occur within made it so – or, at another time, dark and even threatening. Cissie was now quiet and he wondered if it was because she was concentrating on the descent as he too was; it was hazardous enough and it gave him unease to find traces of fencing that he felt should have barred their way. Once again, he had that feeling that he was ever so slightly out of his depth, here in this county so far beyond the environs of the capital, yet at the same time it stimulated him and when they rounded the rocks and his feet touched the sand at last and he stood in the encircled silence, apart from the whisper of the waves, and Cissie stood on her toes and kissed him his doubts flew from him like a startled gull.

They sat on the sort of multi-coloured blanket he would have expected her to bring and ate picnic fare of the Cornish kind. He was amused and delighted to find the eponymous pasty amongst the petite sandwiches with local ham and, when thirsty, she insisted he partook of the elderflower wine that she had made herself; when he had, she kissed him again and, taking up the blanket, she stood and led him to the mouth of the cave. He knew that time could not stand still - he saw that the sun had drifted to the upper rim of the clifftop and a growing wind was beginning to stir the waves from their torpor - but when they had made love, he lay in her arms wishing that it would, and slept.

*

When he woke, his feet were wet.

"It is dry inside the cave, for now," said Cissie from behind him.

Clifton pulled himself back; when next to Cissie he looked outwards to the vanishing sand and at the waves that had crept past the borders of the rocks. The surf beat against the shadowed circle whilst the spray swept upwards and towards him in the now whipping wind and struck him in the face; he tasted the salt. He saw that there was no way back to the path except to swim around the rocks - the incoming tide would soon sweep over them – and hearing the calmness in her voice frightened him as much as this grim prospect. He watched the empty elderflower bottle rock back and forth in the surf and wondered if there was a kind of madness taking place.

"Good God, Cissie, we need to go...*now.*" He stood and in horror watched the sand disappearing before him though the sea was indifferent to their plight; it did not seem possible that the sun, whilst lower in the sky, still shone brightly upon them in the breaks between those clouds moving swiftly across the sky.

"*Now,* Cissie! Do you want us both to drown?"

She remained seated and looked at him calmly. "Not both of us, Raymond..."

He did not understand. How could he? He did not know, until she told him, raising her voice above the growing noise of the wind and the sea, that she had once had a lover, her first, who drowned in this very place. That, when the tide came in, he bid her leave him and save herself as he could not swim, that she had screamed and implored him to try - and he had held her by the shoulders, kissed her, and entered the cave. The choice for her was death or life and she chose the latter because there *was* no choice, not really.

It was then Clifton realised what the young man had meant, that he and others had tried to help her in the aftermath of her despair and guilt. If this was insanity, to take another man that she cared for and relive the moment but with another ending, he

110

strangely understood it - although he still screamed out at her: "Together we can swim, Cissie! Together!"

But she stood, put her arms around him, and kissed him; with her hair loose now, whirling, drawn out and tangled in the squall, she entered the cave.
Clifton looked at its blackness and in anguish cried out her name but, feeling the coldness of death upon him, he chose life, as she had once before, and plunged towards the rocks; and as he swam, the salt from his tears mingled with that of the uncaring sea.

ROUGH DIAMOND

'Why, thank you sir; a dram in these 'ard times is most welcome. The streets is no place to be this time of year, though I've been colder, I 'ave to say. Yes sir, a bite to eat is most welcome too. You an' your missus are angels, sir, an' I reckon if good Queen Vic knew of your kind 'earts, she'd pin a medal on you sure enough. I nearly 'ad one meself once, though the circumstances was somethin' different. It was the Kandahar Diamond that did for me sir…

Tell you about it? Well, it's a tale worth the tellin' I'm sure, though you may not b'lieve what I 'ave to say. Yes, it's a tale alright, but I swear by God it's a true 'un, an' you bein' the kind of man you are may recognise the nature of it: it bein' about loyalty, an' honesty, an' betrayal, an' revenge. I s'pose it's also about love, if you call the kinship we 'ad such a thing.

Who? Well, sir, sit you down on that box over there; take no notice o' them vermin scurryin' about: the brown 'uns is alright. I'll stoke up this 'ere fire an' I'll tell you as you've been kind enough to take an interest. We'll get as cosy as we can under this 'ere arch; we're out of the rain anyways, an' by God you may think it as snug as an 'otel when you've 'eard where I've bin an' what we endured: me, an' Daniel, an' Snudge, troopers of the 60th Royal Rifles an' comrades to the end.

Where to start, sir? That's the thing; if I ramble you'll forgive a worn-out soldier, I'm sure. I *could* begin when the three of us was 'igh in the Bolan Pass an' we took our vow. We scratched it in blood 'cos we 'ad no ink, but I'm of a mind that even if we did, it would 'ave froze before it so much as touched that scrap on which we made our mark: blood was barely 'ot enough. As for our bones, they was chilled to the marrow. Oh, an' our fingers, an' our toes. An' our eyelids: sometimes they was froze tight shut an' we would be turn an' turnabout in leading our little column through the gorges; whoever could see the best at the time fronted it up. An'…but 'old on, I've gone ahead of meself, which 'as always bin my way. I'll light this 'ere pipe, if you have a bit of baccy, sir?

An' your missus, let 'er take a pew too, if she's a mind. There, draw that shawl around you, good angel; that wind is something bitter. Let me begin again.

I was born Tommy Pinter in the backstreets of Bow, an' fairly eddicated on account of my old mum: she 'ad 'er sights set above that of costermonger for me, though a good enough livin' could be made from it, but she 'ated the trade from the time the guvnor set out on his rounds one mornin' an' didn't come back. We found out later 'e'd set up with a floozy in 'Ackney; we was both right pleased when we 'eard she bottled 'im as 'e slept one night an' ran off with 'is dosh. 'E tried to get back in our good books, but I 'ooked 'im one when 'e showed his face at the door; I was sixteen an' above six foot by then.

Before that I was at the 'ragged school' off the Mile End Road. Me mum, with a bit of extra 'elp off the chaplain, learned me to read an' write an' mostly spell right. One thing she didn't count on was me sense of adventure an' when she 'eard 'im telling me tales of musketeers: them as written of by the French gentleman, I forget his name, sir, but you'll know, she gave 'im a flea in 'is ear. I'm thinkin' she could see a sort of light in me eyes, sir, if you know what I mean: 'avin' saved me from walkin' the streets with a barrer, did she want 'er son taking the Queen's shillin' an' trampin' the parade ground or, worse, lyin' stone dead in the mud of some foreign field?

O' course, that was the way of it in the end, as you'll have guessed aright. Mum stood at the door an' barely raised an arm in farewell when I came to say goodbye; I was smart an' strutted like a peacock in me uniform of scarlet kersey tunic an' white leggin's. I could feel 'er eyes on me back as I marched meself away an' when I turned to wave, I could see that arm tremblin' and 'er frame small like a child an' those eyes still starin' but wide an' watery an' frightened – an' I ran to 'er. I felt 'er bones as I 'ugged 'er tight an' wept into 'er neck; I can still feel 'er, sir. I won't forget, though I never saw 'er again, I won't forget me mum…

It was at the City barracks where I first laid eyes on Daniel an' 'Arry, 'im as we all called Snudge. Those two was already thick together, as they came off the same street in Stepney; I counted meself lucky they took to me as much as I took to them. Them six months we was at the barracks, and what a time that was, with the drilling an' the marching an' the roughhousin', made us closer still an' we stuck to each other throughout. God 'elp anyone who got on the wrong side of one of us 'cos the other two weren't far behind; it got so that bullies soon gave us a wide berth.

Not that we were the bullyin' types ourselves sir, please don't think it, though Daniel was four inches taller than me an' stocky with it. He was gentle in the normal course but like a bull when roused, while Snudge was as skinny an' swift as a whippet an' with the same bright eyes: of the two of them, 'e would be the one I'd 'ate to meet in a dark alley in Bow.

What we three 'ad in common though, was somethin' worth more than gold an' what sovereigns can't buy sir: it was loyalty. We struck a sort of oath between us before we was shipped abroad an' it was straight out of that volume that the chaplain read to me: *"One for all and all for one!"* O' course we weren't no French musketeers, but it was a sentiment that all men of arms would welcome; I felt 'appier knowin' I would 'ave 'em at me back in the foothills an' passes of Afghanistan, for that was where we was 'eadin' sir. An' if I'd known then what I know now an' of the 'orrors I'd see an', worse, be a part of, I swear I'd 'ave chucked a dozen Queen's shillin's in the river an' scarpered.

First, there was the journey sir. By now we was billeted down west, then we were steamed off to India under the Raj an' 'avin' never set a foot off land, an' 'appy not to, it was shockin' to me: the swell of the seas made me sick as a dog an' I weren't consoled by knowin' that 'alf the troop felt the same. An' the sailors: 'ow they laughed! I reckon they 'ad the easiest of the journey too 'cos it was us troopers who swabbed an' polished, an' shifted the ashes overboard. What with baccy restricted an' no meal from afternoon till next mornin' an' our 'ammocks 'ung so close they was touchin', we was fair worn out before we docked four months later. It was then that the real 'ell began 'cos we made the long march through the passes straight to Kandahar an' from there onto Kabul.

I'll tell you, by God, it was 'ot by day an' freezin' by night, but we was buoyed by the news of old 'Bobs' (that's General Roberts, sir, an' what a commander 'e was) getting the better of 50 thou' Afghan devils at the Sherpur Cantonment. That bein' just outside Kabul, we knew the city was safe enough for us, but we 'ad to get there first an' 'ere I'll bring in Sergeant 'Awke curse 'is name, 'cos without 'im an' 'is greed an' 'is temptin' ways, I wouldn't be sittin' 'ere chilled an' 'omeless.

'E was 'Awke by name an' 'awk by nature an' with the beak to match, but I'll give the bugger credit: 'e knew how to drive you on, an' when we flagged 'e knew just what to say an' do to make you move, often a kick or a cuff. 'E'd taken a sort of likin' to me an' Daniel an' Snudge ever since the barracks; you might say the Sarge was D'Artagnan to we three musketeers: always pokin' 'is nose in an' not quite one of us, but I think I was the only one of the three who didn't trust 'im from the start. 'E was a fighter though, an' 'ated the Afghans somethin' rotten 'cos of 'is brother goin' under at Charasiab; I'd often see 'im starin' somethin' mad-like at the Hazara tribesman who shadowed us an' when we finally met up with 15 thou' of assorted devils (two for every one of us) at Ahmed Khel, 'e was the one who was whippin' our corps into a kind of cold frenzy an' made sure we kept up a solid volley of fire. It was on a knife edge for a while but Major General Stewart 'ad us mostly well organised an' I will say the Bengalis an' the Sikhs made a good showin' of it alongside the British regulars. After that it was all plain marchin' to Kabul; I'll remember the date though, sir, as 19th April 1880 was the first time I killed another 'uman bein'.

I've said all this, sir, by way of settin' the scene if you like. When you 'ear what I 'ave to say next, I don't want you thinkin' we was cowards when we four did the dirty later 'cos at that same battle I was commended for draggin' Captain Stevens out from under an 'ail of Jezail bullets when 'e was wounded. The Sarge was furious at me for breakin' ranks, but Captain Stevens, 'e said I'd get a medal for it. Meanwhile we made it to Kabul.

It was four months hence when I first laid eyes on the Kandahar Diamond. I called it that 'cos it was where I saw it first, but o' course I 'ad no idea where it came from really an' none of us cared, not much anyway. I only know that from the moment we saw it: me, Sergeant 'Awke, Daniel, an' Snudge, a kind of unreasonin' came upon us an' the path we chose was a downward one, right enough. But let me get on with it, sir; you an' your missus will be feeling chill now an' the night is drawing in quick-like.

We kicked our 'eels in Kabul, with just the odd murderous skirmish outside the walls to occupy us, when we 'eard about the battle at Maiwand. You've 'eard of that, have you sir? Well who 'asn't, 'cos Ayab Khan an' his Afghans overrun 'em all: the 66th Brigade, an' the Bombayers, an' the 1st Grenadiers an' showed the British we wasn't invincible. The survivors fell back to Kandahar under siege; it was then that 'Bobs' led us on that famous march to relieve the garrison there.

It's over 300 miles from one blighted city to the other an' 'Bobs' set us a pace near 20 miles a day in that August 'eat. There was 10 thou' of us, plus followers, an' we was a mixed bunch: Indian native infantry an' cavalry alongside Gurkhas an' the British, 'ighlanders amongst us. Passin' through Ghazni (which means "jewel" sir, believe it or not!) we picked up some Bengal infantry to bolster us up, but we lost men on the way: some was native deserters an' then we had 'undreds a day goin' sick on top. When we finally reached Kandahar, the battle was bloody but compared to the march I thought it was a piece o' me old mum's cake. Ayab had left the city an' made 'is last stand to the west an' we sorted 'im out with not much trouble, so there seemed no reason why 'alf a dozen of our own Ghazni Bengalis took the chance to make a break for the 'ills.

Captain Stevens, 'im who I saved at Ahmed Khel, was furious an' sent us packin' after them; 'e wanted to set an example, I think. There was the Sarge an' we three musketeers an' a couple o' Indian cavalry. The Bengalis 'ad no 'orses an' not much of an 'ead start, so we thought right enough we'd 'ave 'em damn quick and so it proved. We was well up in the foot 'ills though, before we was within firin' range, at which point they took advantage o' bein' above us an' took pot shots. Straightaway one of our men on 'orse went down an' the Sarge was striped along the cheek, what enraged 'im an' 'e made us return fire; that was contrary to orders, as we was supposed to bring 'em back alive.

Well, bein' trained riflemen an' 'avin' the better weapons we brought 'em all down bar one, who at the last knockin's took out our remaining cavalry man with a final shot. When we came up, the Bengali was sittin' with 'is back to a rock an' a kind of sly smirk on his face, what I thought was strange given we was goin' to take 'im back for a court martial an' a probable firing squad.

The Sarge was still 'et up an' all for slittin' Billy Singh's throat, that's what we called the bugger, sir, for we never knew 'is real name, but we three stayed 'im an' I'll always wish we 'adn't.

Billy was one of them noble-lookin' Sikhs with the 'igh brow below 'is turban an' a long black beard, but there was a cunnin' look about 'im an' when 'e reached inside 'is khaki tunic we all made to grab 'im, but 'e shook 'is 'ead an' pulled out a small leather pouch. It was black an' grubby but 'e signalled to the Sarge to put out 'is 'and then emptied something into it: it was a dirty lookin' stone about the size of a pigeon's egg.

Now, I've only seen diamonds on a toff's necklace an' they was all sparkly an' shinin', so I 'ad no idea that what I was lookin' at was a gem worth a small fortune. Only when the Sarge 'ad spat on it an' wiped it on 'is sleeve an' 'eld it up to the sun did I see that it glittered, though I reckon the Sarge's eyes glittered just as much; we was shocked when 'e told us what it was.

I thought to meself that Billy 'adn't done 'imself any favours, oh no. I could see the Sarge's mind workin' on this thought: that if 'e slits Billy's throat now 'e'd have the diamond an' no reply; only 'e weren't sure 'ow we'd take it an' 'e would 'ave to give us fair dibs. Would we be party to murder, sir? That's what 'e was thinkin'.

Billy 'ad an ace up his tunic sleeve though, so to speak, an' in that sly way of 'is told us that there were more diamonds where that came from an' when 'e did, the Sarge's eye's shone shinier than any toff's jewels I'd seen. I looked down on the bloody wreckage of that battle far below an' I suddenly thought to meself I'd 'ad enough. If there was more of that carnage to come, soldierin' weren't what I thought it would be an' it weren't like in the books, an' then there were me mum...what comfort I could give that woman who worked to 'er bones for love o' me an' eddicated me. I wasn't to know that Mum 'ad met 'er Maker 'cos of the cholera; perhaps a broken 'eart sent 'er on 'er way too.

I could see we was all thinkin' on the same lines, sir. Each of the others 'ad a sweet'eart or a mum they wanted to cherish, though I couldn't swear for the Sarge, an' when 'e 'auled Billy up with a curse we gathered the 'orses an' set off up the pass without another word.

We realised it was all or nothin' for us: if we was caught it was the firin' squad, an' if that thought don't make you pick up your feet nothing will. We 'ad our kit with provisions an', with what the 'orses 'ad in their saddle bags, we thought we could get up through the Bolan Pass an' down towards Quetta across the border. We took Billy's word for it you see, sir, me and the lads not 'avin' a clue where we was once we was away from the plains. The Sarge was a bit more canny an' knew the country better than we did but kept 'is eye on Billy just the same. None of us liked the fact that the Sarge 'ad 'old of the diamond though, so *we* kept an eye on '*im*.

Well, I'm goin' to keep this short as I can now, sir, 'cos I can see your missus is shiverin' with the cold an' you'll 'ave a warm 'ouse to take 'er 'ome to, bless 'er.

The upshot is that we kept away from the river what runs through the bed an' the 'igher we went in that damn pass, you'll pardon my language miss, the colder it got an' the more it all looked the same: all bleak an' narrow gorges, although there was the odd, icy stream to keep us in water. An' on the third mornin' when me, Snudge, an' Daniel woke, after we'd all shook an' shivered ourselves to sleep in an 'ollow in the rocks, they was gone. The Sarge, Billy Singh, the 'orses, an' the diamond: all gone, sir, an' us with only what we 'ad on us and few rations left to talk of.

It was blind rage that took us first, then it was panic at our situation an' the last of it was a sort of cold fury; it was then that we took our vow, sir: that bein', we would 'unt 'em down an' kill 'em stone dead or die ourselves in the doin' of it (this bein' the more likely of the two in my 'umble opinion at the time). To seal it we each cut our palms with me knife, an' we dipped the bit of nib I 'ad in blood an' scratched it on the envelope Snudge 'ad kept 'is baccy in. O' course it weren't the whole vow, it were just our names with one word above 'em: that word, sir, was 'Justice'. Snudge an' Daniel was for puttin' it down as 'Revenge', but to me it were justice through an' through an' I made 'em see it my way, though whichever word we chose we knew what we meant by it,

Daniel was the first to go: 'e was a great-'earted lummox an' clumsy with it. Blinded by the frost an' with 'is eyelids 'alf closed, 'e took a sideways tumble over the defile and when we got to 'im 'e was quite dead; 'is face lookin' gentler than I'd seen it in life. Snudge cried like a child, an' why wouldn't 'e? On them Stepney streets they'd played together like brothers. An' I joined 'im, but it didn't stop us takin' 'is coat an' 'is 'at an' anythin' else that was goin' to keep us warm; we knew that Daniel would 'ave it that way. We covered 'im up as best we could an' kept movin'; it was the only thing to do.

Snudge, 'e was too skinny for that cold. 'E froze the next night, though I gave 'im all the clothin' I could, an' when I looked into them bright eyes that was always dartin' an' full of light they was dulled over. I 'ated to see it an' I closed 'em an' then raised meself up. There was only one thought in me mind, one thing that dragged me onward and over until I 'it the path down to the Bolan river: I weren't goin' the way of Daniel or Snudge, not until I 'ad the Sarge's throat in me 'ands or me knife in 'is ribs; I owed it to 'em.

I suppose it weren't a shock to me to find Billy Singh lyin' at the foot of a stream with 'is throat cut. You see, I don't think there was any more o' them diamonds; 'e probably 'alf-inched that one from a merchant in Ghazni, an' who wouldn't lie to save their life? The Sarge, cottonin' on at last, took the one diamond 'e was sure about an' 'e thought 'e was well away; but 'e weren't, no sir.

I was never caught an' I made it 'ome, sir, as you can see; I won't tell you what a wearyin', draggin', roundabout way of settin' foot on this soil I 'ad to take an' the months it took, livin' off me wits an' the charity of others. First though, I gutted the Sarge 15 miles outside Quetta. There now missus, don't you fret; I ain't no murderer, it just 'ad to be done. It just 'ad to...

Now, if you don't mind sir, I'm goin' to bundle meself up; it's the only way to get through the night, but I can see you 'ave your doubts on what I say. 'Ere, take this scrap o' paper an' 'old it up to this match...there, can you see it, sir? 'Justice, Tommy, Daniel, Snudge'. An' you, missus, empty this 'ere pouch into your 'and...you believe me now, oh yes!

I want you to take that diamond, good angels, an' do some good with it 'cos you're the sorts that will. Eh? You don't think I'd better meself with it whilst me fellow musketeers couldn't do you? No, sir, I'll lay me 'ead down an' dream of them two that have gone before me an' if the cold should take me in the night, that won't bother me none either; you see there's me mum, sir, I can't wait to see me mum....'

CHEEK TO CHEEK

It was not a shoe shop, and he did not go in to buy shoes. But then he saw the Derbys, undeniably worn yet buffed with care, and he was drawn to them. They were two tone, of light brown calf leather, saddled with beige canvas on top, and evocative of past sophistication; if they made him think of evenings that comprised dancing and wine and conversation it was not because he himself had experience of such things, rather, they were things to which he aspired.

His full name was old fashioned – Kenneth – and in fact he had once thought of changing it, but he had not enough conviction to believe this would affect his life for the better, so he merely shortened it to Ken. In any event, it was the name that his mother chose and he would not defile her memory; she had given much and if the last absent-minded year of her life was a burden to him when he cared for her alone in Tudor Terrace, Clapham, he had not shown it. Rather, he viewed it as a privilege to feed her and watch old movies with her and make her smile and laugh; these were the last knockings of an unselfish, brought-down and ultimately care-worn life that deserved to be honoured and shared with love and in dignity.

He thought he had misheard her last words. She looked at him gravely but with the vestige of a smile before she finally closed her eyes and whispered so that he could barely hear: "Now…create yourself…"

Of course, she said "*Be* yourself;" anything else would not make sense, would it? But she had held his hand so tightly that afterwards the thought of it impelled him to revisit those words. Yes, perhaps he would 'create' himself anew or, at least, kindle something fresh from the embers of the person he had become in his dull, now middle-aged life. And he was trying; he really was.

Ken admired the shoes, which were set slightly apart and elevated from the surrounding bric-a-brac. The shop was of the small, flea-market type but not devoid of items of interest and even value. He picked the shoes up and looked at the soles.

The small metal tips on heels and toes told him they were for tap dancing and even as he thought this a soft, well-spoken voice said from behind him, as if to elaborate: "They are known as co-respondent shoes."

He turned and smiled at the reason he had entered the shop. She was small in height but certainly not *petite*, and she stood stoutly in front of the counter. Her fair hair was parted in the centre and to his eyes he felt that it would shine were she anywhere else but here, well back from the window where he had seen her setting out wares whilst he meandered dolefully in the winter sun. The sapphire blue eyes, however, were bold enough to be seen in any light and the little confidence he had felt upon entering ebbed away. With her round face and stature, she was not beautiful in her early middle age, but the features he admired were more than enough to make his pulse quicken.

"Oh... er, do you know why?"

She looked and sounded a little vague but, believing it was to do with the corresponding colours on the shoe, she said: "My father is the one to consult really; he is in the rear but is not... hasn't been... himself for a while. He leaves the shop to me now." And before he could politely enquire further, she came towards him and with a: "May I?" gently took one shoe and examined it. "It *is* a beautiful shoe." She admired the brogued brown leather on the uppers and then turned it over to view the worn metal tips. "They have been used of course and many times; this is a shoe that is made for those who love dance..." She paused. "...for those who love life and living it to the full."

She fell silent again, and it seemed to him that, although he did not fully understand the circumstance, her fervent words had brought home the realisation of her own situation: she was minding, possibly tethered to, a small shop of dubious curios, in South London. The sun was shining outside, albeit weakly - and here she was. The Saturday evening would draw in with its promise of gaiety, for some - and here she would remain. He glanced sideways into those blue eyes, which now saw beyond the shoes to something else. They held a look that said there must be so much more – he knew that look because in the small, gilded mirror at home he had seen it himself as he shaved, at the same time humming tunes to which he did not know the names or how they ended.

To hide the unexpected closeness he felt, he peered inside the shoe at a price tag that brought him up and made him blink. "Goodness, why so expensive?"

She looked inside and raised her eyebrows. "I see what you mean... in all honesty, I do not know. Allow me, for a moment..." And she took the shoe and went behind the counter. Her feet trod heavily on wooden floorboarding, a door opened and he heard a chair scrape backwards and the murmur of conversation. He waited rather awkwardly, one shoe in hand, and as he did, he viewed himself in the panes of a tall, French-style display cabinet. The reflection was unkind to him. Something about the glass made him appear even smaller than his five feet eight inches though he could not argue about the tight look of his trousers; rotund may have been one way to describe him, although perhaps too uncharitable given the efforts he had made to lose weight. Nature, in her indifference to any individual's aspirations and desires, had assigned to him a pair of small but protruding ears that supported unfashionable black-rimmed spectacles (without these he would not have been able to see his reflection in the first place). On the plus side, she had allowed him to keep most of his tight, dark hair and all of his teeth. There was a display of capriciousness, however, in giving him a kindly and generous nature, which was in itself something double-edged; his experience was that nice guys found it hard in life compared to those who were driven.

The woman returned and when she put the shoe on the counter, he placed his beside it; their perfect tones attracted him and he idly wondered what size they were. Suddenly, disbelieving what she said even herself, she remarked, "They once belonged to Fred Astaire."

A small tremor ran through him. And yet, he was not surprised that it did; of the many films that he sat through with his mother the musicals of the Hollywood Golden Age were those that energised her. She was soulfully captivated, for in her youth, during the post war years, she had been a fine singer and dancer. "Really? Fred Astaire?" A man who embodied the very elegance and style he sought.

Having just asked why the shoes were so expensive he laughed as he said: "Why so cheap?"

"No provenance, you see? It's just what Dad... my father was told. I suppose it *is* possible they belonged to a famous dancer..." Then she smiled and looked at him. "Or could do..."

"Oh, I think that's unlikely!" He reddened slightly but she continued to regard him, then said quietly: "Why don't you try them on?"

Ken looked down at his feet. They were small – but so were the shoes, and he found himself bending down, undoing his laces. The woman drew up a chair and as he sat and removed his own plain, black loafer shoes, he felt uncomfortable but strangely moved when she knelt and, loosening the Derbys, assisted him in putting them on. With her head bowed, sunlight through the window, still yellow but gradually reddening, suffused her hair from the crown to the ends, brushing her shoulders. Everything in the shop beyond this seemed, to him, to be of contrasting obscurity and no importance. They both stood up together. She seemed smaller, though the heels were of no great height and the shoes themselves felt comfortable, so very comfortable, in fact, that he felt they could not have fitted more perfectly had he visited a store in Oxford Street. He wanted them, though he could not conceive of any occasion in his immediate future when he would use them.

She enquired of him what he thought with a look and raised eyebrows.

"Yes," he said, "yes, I like them, but really they are rather..." He thought of the legacy that his mother had bequeathed, small enough for she had little, but it would be fitting if he could purchase these in memory of her. However, clerking for the council paid badly and it would not do to waste money; there was the rent, bills to be paid...

He took the shoes off without speaking and passed them to the woman, who looked hard at him.

"How much would you pay for them?" she said.

Ken blinked; he was not used to haggling. He thought for a moment and then said the highest figure that he could afford but which was still less than half of the ticket price.

She nodded and, walking behind the counter, reached underneath, bringing out some strong, brown paper. In silence, she wrapped the shoes and tied the package firmly with string. "Make good use of them."

He did not know exactly what to say but when he saw how she looked at him he knew it was incumbent upon him to do what she asked, though he had no idea how; he felt it inside, it was a bargain between them, a mark of trust, and he took the shoes. As he left and walked out into the still bustling street with its stalls and clamour, he merely said: "I will." And for once he believed what he said.

*

Ken had rhythm, but no grace; his mother had told him so, not unkindly, when during his youth she sometimes danced a few steps with him around the kitchen. He had not the frame for it, he knew, but she also told him that although grace came from within, it being a confluence of one's inner rhythm and the music, if it was there, deep inside, it could be brought forth. This he had understood but he did not believe he could ever achieve such a thing. With this still in his mind it was for the first time in his life, a week after he had bought the shoes, that he attended a tap class at the Balham Academy of Dance.

Grander than it sounded, being in a community centre off Bedford Hill, the academy was run by Miss Martin, who was delighted to have a man in her adult class, filled as it was with ladies of a certain age. To be fair, it has to be said that some of them had danced very well in their youth and were returning to this love in retirement.

Dressed casually in brown flannels and a white shirt - he could not bring himself to wear a pair of jazz pants – Ken pulled on his Derbys and stood up, and all the ladies beamed at him with encouragement.

Miss Martin began. "We are going to start with a simple time step…"

At the end of the lesson, the same ladies were still smiling at him but this time with a sense of curiosity, and as he went to leave Miss Martin floated up to him. "Ken! For a first lesson you did marvellously; you are going to fit in perfectly here, I know it. You have such a good sense of rhythm, and… well, style and grace are the words I would use. I hope you will be returning next week?"

Ken looked astonished, then smiled at her. "I will," he said. He looked forward to his future lessons with some excitement.

*

The following year, late on a winter's day, when hanging, leaden clouds spluttered with rain and the cold had cleared the streets of all but the traders and the hardy, the door to an old curios' shop in Clapham was pushed open. An elderly man, seated in a corner behind the counter, looked up absently when the bell jangled. The sound also drew a short, stout woman with fair hair from a room at the back. She placed her hands on the counter top and asked if she was able to help.

"You already have," said the visitor.

"Mary, who is it, Mary?" the old man called from the corner.

The woman saw an angular man, who stood tall and poised in a nicely cut camel coat with a navy suit, and a crisp, white shirt, beneath. His dark hair was short and neat and he had good-natured but determined brown eyes, possibly contact lenses, she thought, which declared to anyone inquiring enough to look that nice guys did not always finish last. He carried a brown paper parcel tied up with string.

"I wanted to give you these. I feel sure that someone will make good use of them."

Something stirred within her and when she had unwrapped the paper to find a pair of beige and brown co-respondent shoes, she looked long and hard at the man. "Well..." she said, smiling.

"Well," he replied, "that's not all." He hesitated only slightly before asking her out. "A dinner and dance," he said. "The dancing is in the grand old-fashioned style, much like the hotel – but I suppose I am slightly old-fashioned myself with a name like Kenneth."

She did not move, but when he saw she had closed her eyes he quickly placed his hands on her own. She did not remove them but eventually looked across at her father, who had risen and was shuffling towards the counter. "I... will have to get someone to look after Dad, but..."

126

The old man had reached them but did not seem to see Kenneth; instead, he rather shakily stretched his hands out towards the shoes. "Now Mary, those are good shoes... don't let *those* go cheaply, my dear."

"No, Dad, I..."

"Gene Kelly wore those, you know." He picked them up and admired them dreamily. "Now *he* was a dancer."

Mary turned quickly towards him. "But Dad! You said..."

For a second Kenneth's legs turned weak, but, catching a glimpse of himself in the same French cabinet as before and in which his reflection now stood elegant and tall, he swiftly put a finger to his lips. Mary fell silent but in any event her father had forgotten them; perhaps in his mind he too swept across a dance floor with a woman in his arms.

"Will I be seeing you later?" Mary asked.

"You will." Kenneth smiled as he left. And as the heavens opened and people stared, he gave not a jot and sang and danced in the rain.

PINCHY HICKS

I suppose I have reached the end of my life without too much in the way of either mishap or misdemeanour. Born in the aftermath of the Second World War, the opportunities for mishap, at least, were few; this was, sadly, not the case for those who fought on our behalf, we children of the '50s and '60s. However, there was a misdeed, an incident minor in itself but deeply affecting to me that, looking back, blots my moral copybook.

It was early in the second decade after that great conflict that I was at my most unruly (I wouldn't go so far as to call myself riotous), although in a naïve and almost inoffensive way; in the drab South London suburbs, where the tiny terraces appeared to house equally small lives, we boys (and the occasional girl) ran shabby and free, unaware of the comedies and tragedies that played out behind those doors, many of which were brightly painted to gainsay their generally colourless aspect and to hint at character, expressing defiance of the dismal world at large.

In my road, at number 32, portly Mr. Price, with his baldness and his twinkling, owlish eyes confounded my parents and the rest of the street by moving in with a smart, permed blonde named Linda; he was never happier, and she, on account of the fact that Mr. Price owned the thriving butcher shop in the small high street, was kept in pork chops and high heels in perpetuity.

It was common knowledge that Mr. Bull, at number 40, beat his wife; feeling his unyielding grip on top of my head as he spitefully clippered my neck (he was the local barber) for the parentally ordered *short back and sides*, it was generally all I could do to prevent myself from trembling. I did so by staring stiffly at myself in the mirror – skinny, dark haired, wide eyed – until he released me, usually with a smirk and a nod.

Mrs. Wright was a widow with a daughter, Kitty, who was, at 13, a year older than I and who played the piano prettily; when she did, I peered through her window from above the sill and watched her hair, golden and hanging to her waist, sway in time to the music; I think I may have loved her then. I did not know that Mrs. Wright wept herself to sleep at the loss of her husband and his income and that the piano would soon be sold.

And then there was Mr. Hicks. I have time left to me, I think...listen to my story of Mr. Hicks, for he burdens my final thoughts.

A meaner, more snappish man we boys, six or seven of us, and Kitty, could not imagine. "Pinchy Hicks" we called him, on account of his penny-pinching ways. For his irascibility, one might argue that he had some justification – his end terrace wall was the perfect goal for our football games, which we loved with an Englander's passion, and with our shrieks and yells from the street outside...well, if I were a grown-up. I guess I'd have felt the same. Therein lies the rub – we were children and not privy to the irritations, and particularly the anxieties, of the adult world – and Pinchy, despite his trade, despised children, or so it seemed.

Pinchy owned the sweetshop and tobacconists of which his terrace was a part – he inhabited the ground floor rear and a small bedroom at the top. I have called him mean – this in the sense of being both miserable and miserly, such that when a football flew over his wall, as it commonly did, it was written off as lost for the chance of it being returned was nil, and the probability of parental support in retrieving it a similarly round figure: "It will teach you to be more careful" was all that was said.

When we had a few pennies on a Saturday, we crowded into Pinchy's shadowy and fusty shop, albeit reluctantly, it being the only one close by with sweets lurid enough to appeal to us: gobstoppers, pear drops, sherbet dabs, fruit salads (6 for half-pence), and blackjacks. The lads tended to be pretty boisterous, picking and fingering the wares if they could (although most were held in bulbous glass jars on shelves behind the counter and well out of our reach), and deliberately scuffling and raising their voices – this to irritate the proprietor as a kind of petty retribution for his meanness. And occasionally I, and sometimes Kitty, would tell the lads to calm down. Here's a strange thing: one would think Pinchy grateful for my intervention, but instead he merely looked at me – eyes dark and intense behind his glasses – as if to warn me to mind my own business. It irked me, though it shouldn't have, and merely strengthened my general conviction that he really was a churlish man. When he had served us our sweets – weighed with precision on the scales, as if to give us one ounce more than we paid for would be the death of him – he would say in a quiet, smoky voice, "Now git art, the lot of you." We were pleased enough to return to the sunlight, dazzling after the interior gloom, and air that smelt all the fresher after the odour of ash and lingering smoke from the cigarette that hung from Pinchy's lips.

Pinchy stepped out to church, St. Saviours, every Sunday, in a brown striped suit – smart with a white collar and tie but shiny at the sleeves - and wearing badly down at heel leather shoes, also brown; his spectacles did not match as their rims and arms were black. He forswore his usual cigarette until his walk back. He looked older than his 50 odd years, and his slightly sparse hair had turned completely grey; but he was upright enough and walked with a curiously dignified gait as he made his way. Oddly, if we saw him upon his return, he invariably looked the worse for his spiritual sojourn – physically, there was a bowing of the shoulders and an expression of downheartedness that made me wonder, if I thought of it at all, what he got out of it. At least on the occasions I was forced to go to Sunday school, we sung a few choruses of "If you're happy and you know it clap your hands." I could not see Pinchy clapping anytime soon. Occasionally Harry, my best mate, would mock him with a shouted, "Cheer up Pinchy – get yourself a new suit!" and he would stop and stare at us; when he turned his eyes on me, I always felt uncomfortable and would nudge Harry, who merely laughed, to get us away.

The evenings seemed longer and hotter in that second decade after the war – summer evenings I mean, when the sun lowered itself at a crawl and the birds sang until bedtime, and the pavement grass verges were yellow and scraggy and tinder-like with the heat. It was on one such evening, when the gang of us had finally separated at the last knockings to head home for tea and bed that I decided to be clever and brave – when in reality, I was merely both arrogant and foolish. Alone and passing Pinchy's yard, I noticed that its door, set in a tall brick wall and streaked and flaking with brown paint, was open – I had never seen it so before, apart from those occasions when a jaded delivery man drew up in his van and offloaded his somewhat mean goods, confectionary notwithstanding.

With the swagger of youth, it struck me how lauded I would be if were to retrieve our footballs – just one would be enough! "What?" they would say, "You actually went into Pinchy's yard!" I could see Harry's grinning face and Kitty's adoring one, and before I could consider further, I had pushed the door and was in.

The yard was shambolic, although no more so than our own backyard at home, and less modest in size than I had imagined. A few cheap wooden crates, empty – some slatted, others not – were piled atop one another; one imagined that the wares themselves were inside a shed, creosoted and with a pitched roof and a door which was secured with a rusted padlock. There were a number of planters and pots holding bright shrubs that surprised me as they contrasted with the general, unkempt air. Of footballs, there was no sign.

I suppose one would think, being aware of those intense eyes and of his demeanour, that Pinchy's yard was not a place to be without permission – a hasty retreat was really in order – but I was a stubborn lad in those days, and curious too; in later years, those traits in fact served me well, in both business and life in general. I decided to take the hastiest of peeks through the rear window of Pinchy's house to see, well, what I could, whether that was footballs or not.

It is always difficult to see into an unlit room through a window from the outside – try it yourself and you will know what I mean – and more so when it is veiled with smut from chimneys that in winter churn their powdered grime out into the streets of the cities; it remains there all year, no rain or cold or sunshine will shift it. So, I wiped the lower of the sashed panes with my sleeve and pushed my face up close.

I could see little of significance, but what I *could* see immediately were three or four balls clustered in a corner of the living room. There was a fireplace of what looked like coloured tiles and a long, shallow sideboard upon which sat several photos and an object just out of view. My thoughts went back to the balls: "Mean sod," I thought, but that was all, because I heard footfall and turned to find Pinchy behind me. Partly because I was scared, but mostly because I knew I was in the wrong, I leapt like a scalded moggy. There was a kind of furiosity about him when he almost hissed, "What are *you* doing here?!"

"Ff...footballs." It was ludicrous, but it was all I could say, and the word came out of me with a kind of splutter; while I watched, he clasped his hands and repeated the word several times as if processing it. When he finally stopped, he looked at me more closely and then abruptly walked past me and, putting the key into the lock of his back door, said in a rough way, "Come in."

Of course, now was the time to get out, my thought being that he wasn't quite all there, and if he told my parents I was on his property, well, that was something safer than being alone with him. At least that was my intention until he turned and said in a tone that was somewhat less brusque than I had ever heard him use, "Come in lad, for Gawd's sake." And taking off his glasses with one hand, he rubbed his eyes with the other; when he looked at me again, it seemed that they were no longer intense at all, merely rheumy and sad.

Today, I don't suppose a child would do such a thing, but in those days, authority was vested in adulthood, and Pinchy's eyes held something that convinced me I would come to no harm – besides, I wanted our footballs – so, putting on a bit of a front, I followed him in.

Well, the interior was dim, and having come inside from the evening sun, it took a few moments for my eyes to adjust, but I could see the room was small and the furniture made it seem even more so: there was a small blue Formica table for eating off of and a stool, an olive wing back chair with a footrest facing the sideboard, and a faded rose cotton curtain that separated all this from what I guessed was a tiny kitchen. It was surprisingly neat; I could still smell ash and the remnants of cigarettes, but this was not unusual in those times. Pinchy sat in the armchair and flicked his head in the direction of the far corner:

"If you want your footballs," he began, but I had turned towards the sideboard and could not help but let out my breath. There, incongruously, was a magnificent ball; it stood proudly upon the sideboard, blown up and taut, splendid with eight brown leather panels. It was slightly smaller than full size and was worn and battered through use but had been buffed with dubbin, and its lace was neatly and tightly tied – it was a football designed for those who could actually play. Besides the football were two photographs and a small silver cup, equally burnished; I leaned over it and read, "St. Saviour's FC, Jonny Hicks, Player of the Year 1954."

"Best they ever 'ad, he was." I looked over at Pinchy as he spoke in a quiet voice, "Best they'll ever 'ave."

I looked closely at the photographs, both in black and white. One showed a team of youths, all of them a couple of years older than me, fit and strong but disparate in their sizes and shapes. They were in two rows, the back standing and the front sitting. Their football boots were lumpen and heavy, and they were in the baggy shorts that were worn back then; some had their quartered football shirts tucked into them, while others had left them hanging loose. It was when you looked at their faces that you saw what they had in common: a winning steel in their eyes, and a joyous confidence – but none more so than the boy who sat in the centre; he was pale, with dark hair parted neatly at the side, and he was laughing as he held the football that was now in front of me.

The second print was of Pinchy – his hair was darker and thicker than now, and he stood tall and proud and smiling, with his arm around the shoulders of that same laughing boy who looked up at him – the football lay on the ground between them.

I reached out and picked the ball up. How I wanted that ball – by comparison, those in the corner now seemed to me a sorry collection – but as I held it, Pinchy quickly stood; he did that clasping thing with his hands again, but this time, he looked at me directly and then at the photos and back again and finally closed his eyes and whispered something.

I strained to hear the words but couldn't and when he opened his eyes, there I stood, with the ball still in my hands. At his look, I went to put it back.

But instead: "Take it," he said in a quiet voice. Then, more loudly, "Take it, lad, take it. Go…go on…git art."

My mouth was open, I could feel it and when I did not move because of the shock of it all, Pinchy shouted, "GIT 'ART!" and I scrambled to the door and pulled it open. When I glanced back, Pinchy was seated, and the little silver cup was in one hand; one convex side reflected a burst of gold and red where the last rays of sunshine had found their way through that solitary clean pane. The other hand was over Pinchy's eyes; his spectacles were on the arm of his chair and reflected the same dying light of the sun. It was the last time I saw him – my last picture of Pinchy.

Who can say what really happened later that night? I had run home and let myself in with the key that hung on frayed string behind the letter box. Darting straight upstairs, I had pushed the ball under my bed, and then, still slightly dazed, went down to our little scullery to eat my tea in silence (an unusual experience for my parents). Only when I had gone to bed and the house was quiet did I retrieve the ball; I held it for a while to make sure it was real – and then I slept.

When a blaze of yellow and crimson accompanied my sudden awakening, my first muzzy thought was that it was still evening and that the startling sky foresaw a glorious morning: "Red sky at night, shepherds delight" – even a South London boy knew that one. Or was it morning already? Yet through the curtains – they were just sheer nets hanging above the sash panes – that light moved with a flickering, swaying persuasion, and there was a clamour outside which, when I threw open the window, was resolved to be that of a milling crowd who were watching with a kind of grimacing horror while a fire engine hosed water upon the burning house at the end of the street; I knew straightaway that it was the sweetshop, and I could see that the water was as ineffectual as the shouts that passed from neighbour to neighbour. I heard Mr. Price asking in a raised voice above the crackle, "Is he in there?!" and my father replying,

"Gawd, yes he is. Bloody 'ell…Eric…Eric, me old son you didn't deserve it."

It affected me to hear Dad refer to Pinchy by his first name, and it struck me for the first time that these neighbours, this community, were close – brought together during, and in the aftermath of, war. I never heard the sigh, but I knew it was there, when Mr. Price replied,

"He went through enough, poor sod."

I leaned out and saw that Mum had one arm tight around Dad's waist and a hand to her mouth – and Mr. Price and Mr. Bull and Mrs. Wright and all the Tom Cobleys of our street stood together as a band, helpless, and watched as the house burned to the ground.

Although our parents had warned us away, the following day, we children stood outside the barrier which protected us from the bricks, mortar, and charred wood that remained; the lead from the grey, slate roof tiles had melted and then solidified into ugly knobs of slag, and although the fire was out, the heat from the ruins could still be felt. Harry took a cursory look, and ever the joker, even in such circumstances as these, turned to us all and said, "Not much chance of getting our balls back now lads eh?" Then to me, "He was a mean old bugger, weren't he?"

Without thinking, I replied, "Oh Gawd, he was tight as a wad." And we all laughed, because in our unease we did not want to confront death and what Pinchy would have suffered. Then I thought of that ball and that cup and that boy, and I wished that I could stop that laughter and take back what I had said. I wanted to shout that we were wrong, that Pinchy wasn't mean at all – but it was too late, and the others had moved away. Only Kitty stayed as I fell silent, and she looked at me curiously until I shook my head. The day moved on, and soon the years, and I never quite forgave myself for the injustice I had done that man who had given me the memory of his lost son. For, as I sat with Mum and Dad that sad evening – who were sombre, if not quite sober, after a couple of G & T's – they told me of Jonny, who had died of polio in '56.

Some said that the grief, eating away at Pinchy, perhaps, had finally burrowed its way so far into his soul that he could stand it no more and set the fire himself. But having glimpsed that soul, I know that Pinchy would not have risked the lives of his neighbours – no, friends – who knew of his loss and in their own unseen ways supported him through it as best they could.

I never married Kitty of course – who marries their childhood sweetheart? – or had a son to whom I could pass on that ball. But I married someone with hair just as long and equally as golden and had a daughter who sits with me now and quietly holds my hand in the failing light.

There…there is that boy with the dark hair, and there is Pinchy, proud as punch. He smiles and nods, and Jonny runs to me for I am returning his ball and we play keepy-uppy with it as children do – except, of course, Jonny is much better at it than I. And I laugh and turn to Mr. Hicks and finally say that I'm sorry.

ABOUT THE AUTHOR

C. G. Harris hails from Kent, known as the Garden of England in the UK, where he loves to read, write, play the ukulele and juggle… almost always not at the same time.

He has a wife, two daughters, three grandchildren, a dog and a cat.

His past exploits have included playing in a rock band, running, and coaching athletes, several of whom have run for GB at junior level.

He is a member of the Sidcup writing group, the Ten Green Jotters, who meet regularly to discuss their literary work and have produced an anthology *Literary AllShorts*.

His first book, *Light and Dark: 21 Short Stories* (also available on Amazon) was shortlisted for the Georgina Hawtrey -Woore Award for Independent Authors 2018, and having completed this second volume of stories, he is now working hard on his first novel: *Billy's Band*.

Printed in Great Britain
by Amazon